Jacob Abbott

Beechnut

A Franconia Story

Jacob Abbott

Beechnut
A Franconia Story

ISBN/EAN: 9783337144289

Printed in Europe, USA, Canada, Australia, Japan

Cover: Foto ©Andreas Hilbeck / pixelio.de

More available books at **www.hansebooks.com**

BEECHNUT.

A FRANCONIA STORY,

Y THE AUTHOR OF THE ROLLO-BOOKS

NEW YORK:
HARPER & BROTHERS PUBLISHERS.
FRANKLIN SQUARE.

PREFACE.

The development of the moral sentiments in the human heart, in early life,—and every thing in fac which relates to the formation of character,—is determined in a far greater degree by sympathy, and by the influence of example, than by formal precepts and didactic instruction. If a boy hears his father speaking kindly to a robin in the spring,—welcoming its coming and offering it food,—there arises at once in his own mind, a feeling of kindness toward the bird, and toward all the animal creation, which is produced by a sort of sympathetic action, a power somewhat similar to what in physical philosophy is called *induction*. On the other hand, if the father, instead of feeding the bird, goes eagerly for a gun, in order that he may shoot it, the boy will sympathize in that desire, and growing up under such an influence, there will be gradually formed within him, through the mysterious tendency of the youthful heart to vibrate in unison with hearts that are near, a disposition to kill and destroy all helpless beings that come within his power. There

is no need of any formal instruction in either case.
Of a thousand children brought up under the former
of the above-described influences, nearly every one,
when he sees a bird, will wish to go and get crumbs
to feed it, while in the latter case, nearly every one
will just as certainly look for a stone. Thus the growing up in the right atmosphere, rather than the receiving of the right instruction, is the condition which it
is most important to secure, in plans for forming the
characters of children.

It is in accordance with this philosophy that these
stories, though written mainly with a view to their
moral influence on the hearts and dispositions of the
readers, contain very little formal exhortation and instruction. They present quiet and peaceful pictures of
happy domestic life, portraying generally such conduct,
and expressing such sentiments and feelings, as it is
desirable to exhibit and express in the presence of
children.

The books, however, will be found, perhaps, after all,
to be useful mainly in entertaining and amusing the
youthful readers who may peruse them, as the writing
of them has been the amusement and recreation of the
author in the intervals of more serious pursuits.

CONTENTS.

———•••———

ENGRAVINGS.

FRANCONIA STORIES.

————◆•◆————

ORDER OF THE VOLUMES

SCENE OF THE STORY.

Mrs. Henry's house at the entrance of a wild glen in Franconia. The time is summer.

PRINCIPAL PERSONS.

Mrs. HENRY, a lady residing at Franconia. Her husband is absent from home.

PHONNY, her son, ten years old. His proper name is Alphonzo, though called generally Phonny.

MALLEVILLE, Phonny's cousin from New York, visiting at Mrs. Henry's.

BEECHNUT, a French boy from Canada, living at Mrs. Henry's. His proper name is Antonio Bianchinette, but the children always called him Beechnut.

WALLACE, a college student, Malleville's brother, spending his vacation at Mrs. Henry's.

MARY BELL, Malleville's friend, residing with her mother in the neighborhood of Mrs. Henry's.

BEECHNUT.

CHAPTER I.

OLD POLYPOD.

PHONNY was impulsive and ardent in his character, and always eager to lead. Malleville was quiet and submissive, and generally very willing to follow. Thus, they agreed very well together, and seldom got involved in disputes; for Malleville was almost always ready to be governed by Phonny's guidance, and to acquiesce in his decisions.

And yet Phonny was often very capricious and changeable. Like other impulsive and ardent boys of his years, he went from one thing to another in his plays, without much reason, or regard to consistency, drawing Malleville with him, when she was his play-mate, as he passed in his caprice from one plan or undertaking to another, each new one being soon abandoned in its turn.

For instance, one summer morning after break-fast, when he and Malleville came out to play, he proposed to Malleville that they should take the garden tools and go out into the garden and weed his border. He had a border in the cor-ner of the garden, which Beechnut had assigned him, and he had sown a great number of flower seeds in it, about a month before the time of which we are speaking. The border was now covered with a very luxuriant vegetation, weeds and flowers having come up together there in great profusion. Phonny had neglected this border entirely since putting the seeds into the ground, but now the idea seemed to strike him that it would be good amusement to go and put it in order. Malleville assented to the proposal. So he went into the barn to get his little wheel-barrow and the tools.

He loaded up his wheel-barrow with a great number and variety of agricultural implements, so as to be sure and have all that he should need, and proceeded toward the garden. Mal-leville followed him, gathering up such tools as fell off from the wheel-barrow as he went along, and dragging them on herself as well as she could after him. Phonny worked upon the garden for a short time—long enough to make a very considerable litter in the walk opposite to his border, by the weeds, with big roots, which he pulled out from among the flowers, and threw down there—and then became tired. He told Malleville that it was a fine day to go a-fishing, and that he thought they had better go down to the pier and fish a little while. In the mean time, he would leave the tools, he said, where they were, and the wheelbarrow; for he was coming back to work in his garden again, after he had rested himself a little while, fishing.

He had some trouble in finding his fishing-line. He looked in the proper place for it, but it was not there. He was sure that he had put it there, he said, when he last used it. Somebody must have taken it away. He went to ask Beechnut if he had seen it anywhere.

"Yes," said Beechnut, "it is round the corner of the house by the well. You left it there day before yesterday when you came home from fishing, and went to the well to get a drink of water."

"Oh yes," said Phonny, "so I did. Now I recollect."

The hook was off from Phonny's line. He had more hooks somewhere, in a box, in the house, but he did not know exactly where He looked in all the probable places that he could think of, and inquired of everybody that he met, but they could not be found. After fretting a little at this vexation, and wishing, somewhat pettishly, " that people would not take his things," he contrived to make a hook of a large pin which his mother gave him, and went down to the pier. He threw his line out upon the water, and then sitting down upon a log which lay upon the pier, he began watching the cork for the indications of a bite. Malleville stood by his side, with her hands behind her, and with *her* eyes fixed upon the cork, very in-tently, too.

Phonny soon became tired of fishing. A boy of his years has, in fact, a feeling of con-tempt for fishing with a pin, which soon be-comes wholly irresistible when the attempt is not successful. So Phonny drew in his line, saying that it was of no use to fish that morn-ing. He did not believe, he said, that there was a fish in the river. Besides, he said, he did not blame them for not biting at a pin.

Phonny's explanations were not very con-sistent with each other, but he was beginning to get somewhat out of humor, and there is nothing that inconsistency so thrives upon as ill-humor.

He drew his line out of the water, wound it up, and went back to the house. There was a wagon standing out in the yard.

"Ah, Malleville," he exclaimed, "here's the wagon. It is just the thing. Let us get in, and have a ride."

He, accordingly, leaned his fishing-pole up against a tree that was near by, and helped Malleville into the wagon. Then he took the long reins and fastened the ends of them to the shafts of the wagon, one to each shaft, as chil dren do when there is no horse, and they wish to make believe drive. He raised the shafts, too, from the ground, and then, with great labor and much tugging, he drew the wagon along toward a wood-pile, and there rested the shafts upon the wood so as to keep them in a horizon- tal position. Malleville was much pleased with being drawn in this manner, and she urged Phonny to go on, and give her a ride in the wagon all about the yard. But Phonny said that she was too heavy.

Phonny then got into the wagon, took the reins and the whip, and then began to drive. He found, however, that the remainder of the harness which was lying upon the floor of the wagon, under his feet, was somewhat in his way. So he threw it out upon the grass. He pretended that the wagon was a ship at sea in a storm, and that he was throwing the cargo overboard. His idea amused both himself and Malleville very much.

When the harness was all thrown out, Phonny gathered up the reins again, and began to drive on, talking all the time in a very rapid manner about the scenery supposed to be in view, and the various objects and incidents which he fancied or invented, as occurring by the way in their imaginary ride. Sometimes he would pretend that they were going through a dark and gloomy wood, and that he was afraid that they would meet with bears or robbers; and he would whip his horses and urge them on with the utmost vigor, to escape from the dangers. Then he would come out into an open country, very rich and beautiful; and would point out to Malleville the streams and lakes and water-falls, or the lofty precipices and the dark mountains which came successively into view. Then he would rein up his horses and stop at the door of an imaginary tavern, and hold long conversations with the landlord about the accommodations which he wanted at the tavern, and the terms on which the landlord would furnish them.

Phonny amused himself and Malleville in this way for about a quarter of an hour, and then he became tired of riding. He got down from the wagon, and helped Malleville down. He looked upon the harness lying upon the ground, with an indistinct idea in his mind, that it was his duty to put it back into the wagon again before he went away; but then he thought that he should come back again pretty soon to take another ride, and in the mean time, that he would go into the work-shop and see what Beechnut was doing.

The work-shop was a large room in a building connected with the sheds and barns, where farming implements were made and repaired; and Phonny and Malleville, having heard a hammering in that direction, while they were in the wagon, rightly inferred that Beechnut was at work there. They found him, when they had entered the work-shop, employed in mending the rakes, in order to be ready for the haying season, which was soon to come on. Beechnut was standing before a great bench. There we e six or eight rakes upon this bench, which

B

18   BEECHNUT.

Beechnut is mending the rakes.   Conversation with him.

Beechnut had brought in to be repaired; and he was now at work upon them, putting a tooth into one, a new handle into another, and a wedge to tighten a loose joint into a third. Phonny climbed up upon the bench, and sat down upon the edge of it, near where Beechnut was working. He also helped Malleville up, and gave her a seat by his side.

Beechnut was just driving in a long wooden peg, which was to form a new tooth for the rake that he was mending.

"Oh, Beechnut," said Phonny, "that reminds me. You promised a great while ago to make me a wooden horse, and you have not done it.'

"Haven't I?" said Beechnut.

"No," rejoined Phonny. "And so you have broken your promise. I don't think you keep your promises well, at all."

"That is a heavy charge to make against me," said Beechnut. "When did I make the promise?"

"I don't know," replied Phonny. "It was a great while ago. You promised to make me a galloping horse."

"And when did I promise that it should be made?" said Beechnut, still going on with his work.

"Oh, I don't know," replied Phonny. "No particular time. You were to make it for me some time or other ; and you have *never* made it, at any time."

" There is more time coming," said Beech·nut "plenty of it. Perhaps I shall make it some time or other yet."

" But you ought to have made it before now," said Phonny. "I don't think you keep your promises at all. Then, besides, I don't think that you always tell the truth."

" Hi—yo!" said Beechnut. " What a char acter I am getting."

" I remember," continued Phonny, " when you were going with us after Carlo, last summer, you told the men along the road, that we want·ed to buy a dog, when we did not wish to buy one at all, we only wished to get back our own.'

" But we wanted to *buy* him back," said Beechnut. " I told the men that we wished to buy a dog, and that was true. We wished to buy Carlo."

" No," said Phonny, " I don't think it was so. And, besides, you deceived them at any rate. You made them think that we wanted to buy some new dog, whereas we only wanted to get back our old one."

"*I* did not deceive them," said Beechnut. "If they were deceived at all, they must have deceived themselves. I told them that we wished to buy a dog. If they inferred from that that it must be a new dog that we wanted, and not any old one, it was their fault that they were mistaken, and not mine. I am sure I did not tell them that it was a new dog."

"But I think you deceived them," said Phonny, "and it is as wrong to deceive any body, as it is to tell a lie."

"Always?" asked Beechnut.

"Yes, *always*," replied Phonny, very positively.

It is generally rather unsafe, to affirm any proposition whatever as *universally* true, since general rules are so extremely liable to exceptions. Phonny thought that he was on very safe ground in making this assertion, but he found in the end, that it was difficult ground to be defended.

"Once I knew a boy," said Beechnut, speaking very gravely, "who had a hen; and as he thought that she would forsake her nest if he took the eggs all out and left it empty, he made a chalk egg, and left it there, for a nest-egg

He wished to make the poor hen think it was a real egg, and so deceive her."

The boy that Beechnut referred to in this case was Phonny himself.

"I know who you mean," said Phonny. "You mean me. But that is a different thing. That was nothing but a hen. I meant that it was always wrong to deceive *men*."

"That was not what you *said*," rejoined Beechnut.

"It was what I *meant*, of course," rejoined Phonny.

"Well, once I knew a man," said Beechnut, "who had only one arm. The other had been shot off in the wars. He found that it was rather disagreeable to other people to see a man walking about with one of his arms off at the shoulder, so he had a cork-arm made with a hand to it, and it was so exactly like a real one that nobody observed any difference. He kept a glove on the cork-hand, and everybody was deceived, and thought it was a real hand."

"*I* could tell," said Phonny; "I know."

"Do you think," asked Beechnut, "that it would be wrong for a man to wear a cork-arm or a cork-leg, so exactly made that people should think it was a real one?"

"I don't think they *could* do it," said Phonny,—"possibly."

"But suppose they could do it," persisted Beechnut, "would it be wrong?"

"Yes," said Phonny, desperately. He did not know how else to get out of the corner into which Beechnut had driven him. "And besides," he added, after a moment's pause, "that is a different thing."

"Different from what?" asked Beechnut.

"Why, from your telling the men in Number Five that you wanted to buy a dog, when you only wanted to find our own."

"So it is," said Beechnut; "I admit it. "And I think myself that it would have been better if I had told them honestly that we had lost a dog, and wanted to find him. And now if you will tell me what my punishment shall be, I will submit to it patiently."

"Well!" said Phonny, "your punishment shall be to go now and make my wooden-horse."

"It shall be done," said Beechnut, "as soon as I have finished this rake."

Accordingly, as soon as Beechnut had completed the repairs of the rake that he had in hand, he conducted Phonny and Malleville out into the shed to look at a great log which he had laid aside some time before for the body of the wooden-horse. It was a log of a very irregular shape, bearing, however, some rude resemblance to a horse. Beechnut had observed this odd conformation of the log as it lay in the wood-pile the winter before, when he was cutting up the wood, and had, accordingly, thrown it aside, intending to put legs to it some day or other for Phonny; but the convenient time for doing it had not arrived until now.

"There," said Beechnut, as he pointed out the log to Phonny and Malleville. "What sort of a horse do you think that will make for you?"

"Most excellent," replied Phonny. "Haul him, and put his legs in immediately."

So Beechnut and Phonny pulled the log out, and after tumbling it over and over two or three times, so as to get it out where they all could stand around it to take hold of it, they lifted it up, and, with great labor, lugged it into Beechnut's shop. Malleville tried to help in the work by taking hold of a sort of branch which represented the tail, and lifting at it with the little strength which she had at her disposal. Thus the monster was finally got into the shop, and tumbled down there upon the floor.

Beechnut then began to make the legs for

the horse, and to bore holes with a great auger, in the body, for the insertion of them. While he was doing this, Phonny asked what name his horse should have when he was finished.

"I don't know," said Beechnut. "You must name him yourself. You can't call him a quadruped, for he is going to have more than four legs."

"What is he going to have more than four legs for?" asked Phonny.

"So as to make him a galloping-horse," replied Beechnut. "If I make six or eight legs, and have them of different lengths, you can rock him back and forth, on his various legs, and so suppose that he is galloping. You had better go and ask Wallace what would be a good name for an animal with six or eight legs He will find out by his Latin and Greek."

"Well," said Phonny, "I will."

"Or no," said he again, after a moment's thought. "It will be better for you to go, Malleville: because you see I want to stay and see Beechnut finish the horse."

"But I want to stay too," said Malleville.

"Why, that isn't of so much consequence," argued Phonny. "You see it is necessary for me to know how horses are made, for perhaps

I shall have to make one myself some day. I may want to make a little one for you, if I can only find a log next winter. So it is better that you should go and ask Wallace about the name."

Malleville was easily persuaded in such cases as these, and though she had no great confidence that Phonny's plan of making a horse for her would ever be accomplished, she consented to go and do the errand to Wallace. In due time, she returned.

As soon as Phonny saw her coming, he called out to know what Wallace had said.

" What is his name to be ?" said he.

" It is Polly something," said Malleville. " He has written it down on this paper."

Phonny took the paper, repeating at the same time the name which Malleville had suggested in a tone of contempt.

" Polly !" said he. " Polly is no name for a horse."

So Phonny opened the paper, and read what was written within it, aloud to Beechnut and Malleville, thus :

" If he has six legs, call him Hexapod. If he has more than six, I think you had better call him Polypod."

Phonny threw back his head and laughed aloud.

"Oh, Polypod!" he exclaimed. "What a name! Oh, Mollypod!"

The legs of the horse were soon finishea They were formed of short poles sharpened a little at one end, so as to be driven firmly into the auger-holes which had been made to receive them. They were set in such a manner as to *spread* a little laterally, so as to prevent the horse from falling over upon his side. The egs, too, were of different lengths, the middle ones being a little longer than those extending before and behind, so that when a rider was seated upon the horse, and rocked him to and fro, a sort of jolting motion was produced, which Phonny called galloping, and which he and Malleville found very agreeable. When the work was done, they carried the horse out to a place where there was a solid plank platform at the end of the house, and established him there. Beechnut brought out two buffalo robes from the barn, and folding them twice, he placed them upon the horse, one behind the other. The foremost formed a saddle for Phonny, and the other a pillion for Malleville. It happened that there was a sort of branch grow-

The children mount the wooden horse.

ing out of the log, between Malleville's seat and Phonny's, which was very convenient for Malleville, to enable her to hold on. When all was thus ready, Beechnut taught them a song to sing, which he made up for the occasion, and then he went away, leaving the children singing and riding old Polypod, keeping time by their music, with the jolting of the horse.

OLD POLYPOD.

The song was this:

"High and low,
Fast and slow,
Over the hills away we go.

Round and square,
Up in the air,
The birds are singing, Begone dull care.
Hie, old Polypod! Ho, old Mollypod!
Fumbling, rumbling, stumbling Polypod."

The children sang this stanza with great glee,
and at the top of their voice, adding every time
they came to the end of it, a chorus of loud and
long-continued shouts of laughter.

About two hours after this, Beechnut, in looking about the yard and garden, found the traces
of disorder which Phonny and Malleville had
left in the walk opposite the border in the garden, and about the wagon in the yard. He put
the things which Phonny had left out of place,
properly away, and noted the time which it required to do so. The time was ten minutes.
He then went in search of Phonny.

"Well, Phonny," said he, "how do you like
old Polypod?"

"Very much, indeed," answered Phonny.

"Have I fulfilled my promise now, to your
satisfaction?" continued Beechnut.

"Yes," said Phonny, "entirely."

"And did I submit to my punishment, for not
telling the exact truth to the men in Number
Five, with a good grace?"

" Yes," said Phonny.

" Now," continued Beechnut, " I have a charge against you. You have been at work in the garden, and you left the wheelbarrow, and the tools, and ever so many weeds, in the walks ; and then you went to play in the wagon, and finally left it out of its place, and with the reins tied to the shafts, the harnesses on the ground, and every thing in confusion."

Phonny appeared quite astounded at these heavy accusations. He did not know what to say.

" Are you guilty or not guilty ?" said Beechnut.

" Why guilty, I suppose, replied Phonny, " but I will go and put the things right away."

" No," replied Beechnut, " that is done already. " Every thing is put away excepting your fishing-pole. That is your property, and I have nothing to do with it. The garden and the wagon, it is my business to take care of, so I have put them in order, and all you have to do is, to submit to the proper punishment for putting them out of order."

" Well," said Phonny, " I will. What is the punishment ?"

" You must pay double damages," said Beechnut. "It took me ten minutes to put the things away, and you must do work for me, equal to twenty minutes. But then, as your time is not worth more than half as much as mine, it will take you forty minutes to do the work."

"Well," said Phonny. "What is the work to be?"

"Turning the grindstone for me to grind the scythes, after tea," said Beechnut.

Phonny made no objection. In fact, he went to his work so good-naturedly, and was so industrious in doing it, that Beechnut released him at the end of half an hour.

Beechnut never scolded; he always punished the boys that he had dealings with, for their faults and delinquencies. It is true, the boys were not obliged to submit to his punishments, but they generally did so of their own accord, for the punishments were always reasonable and just, and Beechnut was, moreover, very good-natured, though still very firm, in inflicting them. Sometimes his punishments were of a very odd and whimsical character, and afforded great amusement,—while yet they answered the purpose of punishments perfectly well. They were sometimes, too, in name and form at least, pretty severe. He once actually

hung a village boy, for some rebellion agains,
his authority. He hung him to the limb of a
tree. The only material difference between
the hanging of this boy, and a regular execu
tion, was, that the rope in the boy's case, in
stead of passing round his neck, was put unde
his arms.

CHAPTER II.

THE GREAT BLACK BEAR.

THERE was another promise that Beechnut had made to Phonny and Malleville besides the one in relation to the wooden-horse, which for a long time he postponed fulfilling. It was the promise to relate to them the incidents of his early life in Paris, and the circumstances by which his father had been led to come to America. The reason why this story had been so long postponed was, that Beechnut said it could not be well understood without having his picture of Paris at hand, to look at the places which he should refer to in his story. Beech-nut had a large and handsome picture of Paris hanging up in his room. He had brought it with him from Paris, when he came to America, together with a great many other similar treasures. These things had all been left at Montreal, when Beechnut and his father came across through the woods from Canada to the United States, but Beechnut had sent for them afterwards, and had safely received them. By

means of these treasures Beechnut had contrived to make his room in Mrs. Henry's house
a very attractive place; and among the various
objects of interest and curiosity which he had
collected there, not the least alluring was his
large colored picture of Paris which hung up
in the room in a conspicuous position. This
was the picture that he referred to as essential
to a right understanding of the story of his
early life.

Although Beechnut's room was, as we have
said, a very attractive place, still he spent very
little time in it, being occupied generally during
all the hours of every day in his work about
the house and farm. There were the evening
hours, it is true, but during the summer the
evenings were very short, and during the winter it was too cold in his room to remain there
long. There was indeed a fire-place, but
Beechnut never had a fire in it, or at least very
seldom. It happened thus that he spent very
little time in his room, and no convenient op
portunity occurred for being there with Phonny
and Malleville so as to sit opposite to the picture
of Paris and hear the story. In fact, it is im-
possible to say how long it would have been
before such an opportunity would have been

presented, had it not been for a certain great
black bear.

It may seem extraordinary that there should
be any connection between Beechnut's oppor-
tunities for story-telling and the movements of
any bear. But so it was. The way in which
it happened was thus :—

A large black mother bear that had been
living for some time with other bears in remote
regions among the mountains, at length about
the middle of the summer became tired of the
dismal solitude of her abode, or else perhaps
she found it difficult to obtain food enough in
the woods for her young cubs, which having
become pretty large wanted a great deal to eat.
The old bear came, accordingly, through the
woods toward the settlements of men, to see
what she could find there. She was very successful in this expedition. She found a flock
of sheep sleeping quietly at midnight in a lonely
field near a farmer's log house. The bear crept
up slily to the place and seized a lamb in her
monstrous jaws, and then ran off into the
woods again. The lamb set up a loud and in-
cessant bleating in its agony of terror, though
the sound of it grew fainter and fainter as it
was borne off through the thickets. The whole

flock of sheeep was aroused by these sudder cries, and all began to bleat too, and to run in a dreadful panic toward the house, to alarm their master. They all ran thus except one, the mother of the lamb that was carried away. She, instead of flying toward the house, ran toward the dark and gloomy thickets where her lamb had so mysteriously and dreadfully disappeared, determined to attack the unknown enemy with the utmost fury, if she could overtake it, whatever it might be. She, however, could not overtake it. The bear knew perfectly the way that she was to go. She had eyes, too, that enabled her to see her way, even through the densest recesses of the forest, and in the darkness of midnight. The sheep, on the other hand, was soon bewildered and lost, and ran to and fro in an agony of distress and terror.

The farmer came out with a lantern to discover the cause of this commotion, but he could not ascertain any thing satisfactory. He supposed, however, that some wild animal had come from the woods and frightened the flock, but he could not determine whether any of the sheep or lambs had been carried away. The darkness and the confusion prevented him from counting those that remained, to see if all were there. He presumed, however, from the bleat-ing of the mother-sheep above referred to, and from the other symptoms of distress which she manifested, that one of her lambs was gone.

In the morning all doubt was at once re-moved, on the first survey of the ground; for the spot where the bear had struggled with her prey was plainly to be seen, and her track could also easily be traced into the thickets, marked, where the ground was soft, by the impression of her own footsteps upon the pathway, and at other places by blood.

On making these discoveries, the farmer's indignation was aroused to the highest pitch against the bear.

" The bloodthirsty wretch!" he exclaimed " What a cruel monster to carry off and butch-er a poor innocent lamb like that!"

There was, however, no just cause for this indignation—certainly not on the part of the farmer himself,—for he was rearing this very lamb for the identical purpose to which the bear had appropriated it, namely, to kill it for food for his family. He had the very day before killed another of his lambs, and roasted a part of it before the kitchen fire, to make a dinner for his children Men often exhibit this same kind of unreasonableness in censuring one another. They condemn very severely in their neighbors, things which they do themselves without any compunction.

Unreasonable as it was, however, the farmer was extremely indignant. He left the tracks which the bear had made, just as they were, and called his neighbors in to see them. The neighbors were indignant too; and as they had flocks and herds which were in the same danger, they soon formed a plan for arming themselves, and setting off into the woods in a company, to endeavor to intercept the bear in her retreat, and kill her.

For arms, the farmers got out all the muskets, fowling-pieces, and pistols that they could find in their houses; and those who had nothing that would shoot, supplied themselves with pitchforks, hatchets, and great clubs. One man made a sort of spear of the point of a scythe, which he contrived to fasten into the end of a handle that had once belonged to a pitchfork. He cut away a part of the blade of the scythe with a cold chisel, so as to form a sort of shank which could be driven into the handle. It made a very formidable looking weapon, indeed. When it was finished, the man brandished it in the air before him, and said that all he wanted now, was to see the bear coming at him with her mouth open, and he would give her something to swallow not quite so tender as the flesh of that lamb.

In the mean time, the messengers who had been sent abroad, galloped from farm-house to farm-house, spreading the tidings. One of them came to Mrs. Henry's, and told Beechnut the news, in hopes that some of Mrs. Henry's workmen might go with them. It happened, however, that these workmen were all away. At the time when the messenger came to the house, Phonny was down by the river, upon the little pier, fishing. Malleville was just going down to join him, but her attention was arrested at seeing the horseman ride rapidly into the yard; and when he stopped before Beechnut, who was saddling the horse at a post near the barn, she walked up to the place to hear what was the matter. After telling the story to Beechnut, the horseman rode away as fast as he came. Beechnut left the saddle, loose, upon the back of his horse, and hurried into the house. Malleville walked slowly and thoughtfully down toward the pier, thinking of the bear and the lamb, and intending to tell the story to Phonny.

Phonny had heard the footsteps of the horse, as he came galloping along the road, and so had looked round to see what was the matter. He observed that the horseman, after a moment's conversation with Beechnut, went galloping back again as fast as he came. This excited his curiosity. He stood, accordingly, upon the pier, holding his fishing-pole in his hands, with the line in the water, but with his face turned away from it toward Malleville, thus watching her as she approached, instead of looking for a bite at the end of his line. As soon as Malleville came near enough to be heard, he called out to her, saying,

"Malleville, what was it that that man galloped into our yard about?"

"About a bear," said Malleville.

"What about a bear?" asked Phonny very eagerly.

"It is about a bear," exclaimed Malleville, coming now pretty near to Phonny, so that she could speak in her ordinary tone of voice, "that came out of the woods and carried off a poor little lamb. The men are all going off into the woods to shoot the bear, and bring the lamb home again."

"Are they?" said Phonny eagerly.

Immediately, in a very hurried and excited manner, he laid his fishing-pole down upon the pier, placing a flat stone across it 'o keep it steady, and set off toward the house. Malleville ran after him, urging him to wait for her. He was running so fast, that she could not keep up with him. Phonny, however, was too much excited by the intelligence which he had received, to pay any heed to Malleville's calls. He made his way, as fast as he could, into the yard, to find Beechnut. He caught a glimpse of him going into a back shop. Phonny followed him there, and found him examining an old gun which he had taken down from a high shelf there.

"Are you going into the woods to shoot the bear?" asked Phonny.

"I am going into the woods," replied Beechnut, "but I do not expect to shoot the bear."

"Has my mother given you leave to go?" asked Phonny.

"Yes," replied Beechnut. This was true. Beechnut had been into the house and had informed Mrs. Henry of the circumstances of the case, and had asked permission to accompany the expedition into the woods. Mrs. Henry had been at first entirely unwilling to give her consent that he should go. But Beechnut said that *they* had flocks of sheep to be defended as well as the neighbors, and that it was incumbent on him, since all the men attached to the farm were away, to be ready to go with the other farmers, and, whatever might be the difficulty or the danger, to take his share of it with the rest. So Mrs. Henry finally consented.

"I mean to go, too," said Phonny. "I will go and ask my mother."

So Phonny ran off to the house. In a few minutes he returned again, looking very downcast and disconsolate. Beechnut was still at work upon the gun. His attention was wholly absorbed by it, so that he paid no attention to Phonny. Malieville was standing by looking at the gun with an expression of mingled curiosity and awe.

"Will she let you go?" asked Malleville in a very gentle voice.

"No," said Phonny, peevishly. "And I **don't** see why. *I* might go as well as Beechnut."

"She will not let you go then?" said Beechnut, snapping some part of the gun back and forth in his attempts to put it in order.

"No," said Phonny, speaking in a very fretful tone.

"How provoking!" said Beechnut.

"Yes," rejoined Phonny, "it is provoking indeed."

"And how unreasonable!" said Beechnut.

"Yes," responded Phonny.

"If I were you I would not bear it," said Beechnut.

"Why, what would you do?" asked Phonny.

"Oh, I don't know," said Beechnut. "I would do something or other very desperate. I would fret about it all day."

Phonny was silent.

"You will not find another thing so good to fret about in a twelve-month," continued Beechnut. "It is astonishing what trials and straits innocent boys are put to by hard-hearted mothers. Here now is a boy that his mother will not allow to set off in a company of fifty men, with dogs and guns, to make a tramp of six miles through the woods and mountains hunting a wild beast,—and he bears it, dear little fellow, as patiently as a lamb!"

So saying, Beechnut began to pat Phonny gently on the back.

Phonny seized a leather strap, a part of an old bridle which chanced just then to be lying

on the bench, and gave Beechnut a great
whack across the shoulders with it, and then : an
off out of the shop.   He tried very hard to look
cross until he had got out of sight, but he could
not quite effect it.   He burst into an invol-
untary and distressing laugh just as he was
passing the door.   But he recovered himself
almost immediately, and Beechnut having put
up the gun, and followed Phonny to the door,
saw him standing there pretty near, and looking
as sullen as ever.

"Poor little lamb!" said Beechnut in a tone
of great condolence.

Phonny ran at Beechnut on hearing these
words, to pound him with his fist, but Beechnut evaded him by running round the horse,
and thus keeping out of his pursuer's way.
He also said by way of deprecating Phonny's
displeasure :

"I meant the lamb that the bear carried
away—not you."

"No," said Phonny, "you meant me.   I
know you did "

Beechnut watched his opportunity while
dodging about the horse to put the saddle properly on, and to fasten the girth.   He then suddenly retreated into the shop, and came out a

44 Beechnut.

Beechnut determines not to take the gun. His reasons.

moment afterwards with his mountain-axe, which was a small and light axe, though the handle was as long as that of any other axe. With this axe in his hand, he mounted the horse and began to ride away.

"Are you not going to take the gun," asked Phonny.

"No," replied Beechnut.

"Why not?" asked Phonny.

"Oh, there are various reasons," said Beechnut. As he said this, he was advancing rapidly upon his horse across the yard toward the gate, Phonny trotting along by his side, and holding on by the stirrup. "There are various reasons," said he. "It is out of order, and I am afraid it would not go off; and if it should go off, I am afraid it would kick me over; and if it did not kick me over, I am afraid it would shoot some of the men; and if it did not shoot any of the men, I am afraid it would not hit the bear. And besides all that, there is David's reason for taking a sling and not a sword, when he went out to fight Goliah. He *knew* the sling, and he did not know the sword. I *know* my mountain-axe, and I don't know any gun. So good-bye. Poor little lamb!"

Phonny ran out to the road-side and seized a

handful of grass to throw at Beechnut as he can-
tered away, and then walked back to meet Malleville. He told Malleville that Beechnut was
the greatest teaze that ever he knew, and he
hoped that the bear would catch him in the
woods and eat him up.

Phonny then went and got a wooden gun
which Beechnut had made for him some time
before, and amused himself and Malleville for
more than two hours in rambling about the
yards and gardens, and shooting at various objects which he made, in his imagination, answer
as representatives of bears. The fishing-pole,
which he had left upon the pier, was entirely
forgotten.

Beechnut was brought home about the middle
of the afternoon of that day quite seriously hurt.
The manner in which this accident befel him
was as follows :—

The party of men that were to go out to hunt
the bear met at an appointed place of rendez
vous near the house of the farmer whose flock
had been attacked. Here they agreed upon
the rules of the expedition. They were all
to proceed together, following the track of
the bear, as long as the track could be seen
Then they were to separate into different par,

ties, each under its own leader, and proceed by different paths though in the same general direction. They were all to be very carefu not to fire a gun unless they should actually see the bear, so that the report of a gun heard in the woods would be an imperative signal that all who should hear it must repair immediately to the spot from which the sound came. In case the several parties should become too widely separated to hear the reports of the guns, if occasion should occur for firing them, or in case the bear should not be seen by any one, and so the guns not be fired, they were each to go on as far as they thought they could safely go and get back that night. These arrangements being all formally agreed upon, the expedition commenced its march.

The men went on without any particular adventure for more than a mile, following the track of the bear, which they succeeded in tracing for this distance. Sometimes they lost it for a moment, but they soon recovered it again, and went on. The men walked in single file, with the more experienced and sagacious hunters in front to watch for the track. Some of the young men in the company laughed at Beechnut for bringing an axe. They asked

him whether he expected that an old she bear
was going to stand still like a maple-tree while
he came up with his axe to cut her down.
Beechnut took all this raillery in very good part,
and trudged patiently on in his place in the line,
with the axe upon his shoulder.

After getting about a mile and a half into the
woods, the leaders of the party lost sight of the
track and could not recover it again. The
company then divided into several distinct parties and went on at a little distance from each
other so as to explore a considerable breadth of
forest as they advanced. The party to which
Beechnut was attached consisted of about six
men. The leader of this party was an old and
experienced hunter, whom the men called Uncle
Harry. Beechnut joined this division because
he had more confidence in Uncle Harry than in
any of the other commanders. The rest were
noisy and talkative, but Uncle Harry was quiet
and still, and yet very observant and watchful;
he said but little and made no pretensions, while
the others were continually calling out to the
company to go this way and that, and direct-
ing their attention to discoveries which always
turned out to be nothing in the end. Beechnut
observed all these things, and concluded that

there would be the best chance of seeing the bear in following Uncle Harry.

He was right in this conjecture. Uncle Harry knew the whole country perfectly well, and he formed a perfectly correct judgment of the route which the bear would be likely to take. He went on, however, without making any discoveries, for more than three miles, passing over and through all sorts of difficulties and obstacles, which cannot be particularly described. At ength, just as he was entering a wild and dismal glen, almost surrounded by rocky precipices, he suddenly stopped, and said,

" Hush !"

He pointed up the glen. The men all looked, and there, upon the ground, under a large oak-tree, they saw a monstrous black bear sitting up and looking at them with fierce and glaring eyes. A moment afterwards they heard a long low and angry growl.

Beechnut immediately looked all around the glen to see if there was any way by which the bear could escape from them in case she was attacked by the men and wounded. He saw that there was one path leading up the rocks upon one side of the glen, which seemed to afford the only egress. He immediately left the

THE GREAT BLACK BEAR. 49

Conflict with the bear.   Beechnut and his axe.

party, and running into the thicket, he stole round in a circuit until he came out to this path, about half-way up the ascent. Before he reached this point, however, he heard one volley discharged from the guns.

When he reached the path, he sheltered himself behind a great tree that was there, and then peeping out upon one side he looked down into the glen. The bear had disappeared. She had been slightly wounded by one of the guns, and had scrambled up into the oak-tree. The men were loading their guns anew. Presently they fired a second time. The bear was slightly wounded again, and terrified at the noise made by the guns and at the smoke and fire, she came down the tree with great impetuosity and rushed toward the path which Beechnut was guarding. Beechnut stood all ready with his axe as she came climbing up the steep path, and at the instant that her head came within his reach he dealt upon it a tremendous blow, and felled the bear to the ground. He immediately began cutting off her head with rapidly repeated strokes of the axe, and before any of the men could reach the place the head was severed completely from the body.

The report of the guns and the shouts of the

D

men brought up one of the other parties to the
spot. The rest had wandered too far away to
hear them. The men who assembled made a
sort of hand-barrow of the stems of young and
slender trees, to put the carcass of the bear
upon, and carry it home. They found a road
in returning which took them back by a nearer
way than that by which they came. When
they began to approach the settlements of the
farmers, Uncle Harry and the other men insisted that Beechnut should get upon the bar-

BRINGING HOME THE BEAR.

row too, that they might carry him home in triumph. Beechnut wished to decline this honor, but the men all absolutely insisted cn his compliance. So he mounted upon the bar row, and took his seat upon the bear.

The procession went on very well in this way for a short distance, but at length they came to a little bridge, which, though strong enough for ordinary travel, could not bear this great load, consisting, as it did, of the bear and Beechnut, and the men that were carrying them. The bridge broke down, and half of the party fell into the brook. Beechnut, being the highest, fell the farthest, and the sharp end of one of the poles of the barrow entered his leg and made a shocking wound.

For the rest of the way he had to be carried in earnest, and he arrived at home at last, in the condition in which great heroes so often find themselves—covered with glory, but tormented with pain.

Another of the disasters of the day was, that Phonny lost his fishing-line. A large fish bit at his hook while he was in the yard with Malleville shooting imaginary bears. The fish was strong enough to pull the fishing-line, pole, and all into the river, notwithstanding the flat stone which Phonny had placed over it, to secure it. Phonny went down in the course of the afternoon to get his pole and line, but they were gone, and he could never find out what became of them

BEECHNUT'S PICTURE OF PARIS. 53

Pain of Beechnut's wounds.   He wants water.

CHAPTER III.

BEECHNUT'S PICTURE OF PARIS.

FOR two or three days Beechnut suffered a great deal of pain from his wound. He was feverish and restless besides, and very thirsty all the time. Phonny and Malleville went in sometimes to see him, but he could not talk much with them, and so they soon went out. Phonny went up to the bed-side at one time and asked Beechnut whether there was not any thing that he could do for him. "Yes," said Beechnut, "if you will just go up into the mountains and bring me down a little brook, so that I can have it running here by my bed-side, and drink as much as I want, I will be everlastingly thankful to you."

Phonny laughed, and said that he could not do that; but he would go down to the well and get him a pitcher full of cool water. Beechnut replied that that would not do him any good; for if Phonny brought the water, they would not let him drink it.

" Won't they let you have any thing to drink ?" asked Phonny.

" Very little," said Beechnut.

Phonny had the opportunity very soon after-wards to see *how* little they gave Beechnut to drink, for the nurse came to the bed-side and asked him if he was thirsty. Beechnut said he was. So the nurse took up a little water in a tea-spoon from a tumbler which was standing upon a small table at the bedside, and put it to Beechnut's mouth. Beechnut took the water, and then turned restlessly over and shut his eyes. Pretty soon after this Phonny went away.

Two days afterwards Phonny and Malleville came to Beechnut's door one morning after breakfast, and peeped into the room. Beech-nut saw them, and called out to them to come in. As they entered, they perceived at once that his whole appearance was changed. His coun-tenance was beaming with health and happi-ness.

" How do you do this morning?" said Phonny.

" WELL," said Beechnut, emphatically, swinging his arms at the same time over his head. " Well. Perfectly well I never felt better in my life. I could mow an acre of grass this morning as well as not, if they would only bring it to me here upon the bed. And I am going to have beef-steak for breakfast Think of that!"

Phonny said he did not think *much* of that. He had had beef-steak for breakfast himself every morning for a week.

"But I am a convalescent," replied Beech-nut. " The greatest happiness in the world for a boy, is to be a convalescent and to have beef-steak and a cup of coffee for his breakfast."

"Only," continued Beechnut a moment afterwards, in a saddened tone, " I have got to be still on this bed a week longer, till the wound gets healed."

Beechnut then attempted to sit up in his bed a little by way of showing how strong he was. He found, however, that he was not so strong as he had supposed. In fact, he felt very weak, and on attempting to raise his head he became faint and giddy. He was therefore very glad to lie down again.

He, however, gained a great deal of strength in the course of the day. Phonny and Malleville came in several times to see him, and in the afternoon he was well enough to hear

Phonny read a story from a book; only Beech-nut got asleep during the reading. Phonny looked a little disappointed when he turned round at the most interesting part of the story and saw that Beechnut was asleep; but the nurse seemed pleased, and said that she was very glad. The very best thing, she said, that could be done with a book in the case of any one who was sick, was to read him to sleep with it. If it were not for that effect of reading, she never, she said, would allow a book to come into a sick chamber.

After his sleep Beechnut felt quite rested and refreshed; and Phonny, happening to cast his eyes upon the picture of Paris which was hanging upon the wall not far from the bed, in such a position that Beechnut could easily see it as he lay with his head upon the pillow, reminded Beechnut of his promise to tell them about Paris at some time, and about his early life there. Beechnut said that he would perform his promise that very evening after tea. Accordingly, after tea Phonny brought Malleville up into Beechnut's room to hear the story.

The head of the bed upon which Beechnut was lying was at one end of the room not far from a window. The picture of Paris was

hanging over the fire-place which was opposite
to one side of the bed.   The window was between the bed and the fire-place.   Near the
head of the bed, and between it and the window, there was a great " easy chair," as it was
called.   It was large, and was very comfortably
lined and stuffed.   It belonged in Mrs. Henry's
room, and had been brought into Beechnut's
room that he might sit in it as soon as he should
be able to sit up.

When Phonny and Malleville came in to
Beechnut's room to hear his story, Malleville
took possession of the easy chair and established
herself there.   Phonny climbed up upon the
bed and sat with his back against the foot-board.
Thus he could look toward Beechnut while
Beechnut was talking, and could also see the
picture at any time by turning his head a little
toward one side.

When they were all ready, Beechnut began
as follows.

" There is a river that runs through Paris.
The name of it is the Seine."

" Yes," said Phonny.   "I knew that Paris
was on the Seine.   I learned it in the Geog-
raphy."

" You can see the river in the picture," said

Beechnut, pointing to the picture, but taking no notice of Phonny's interruption.

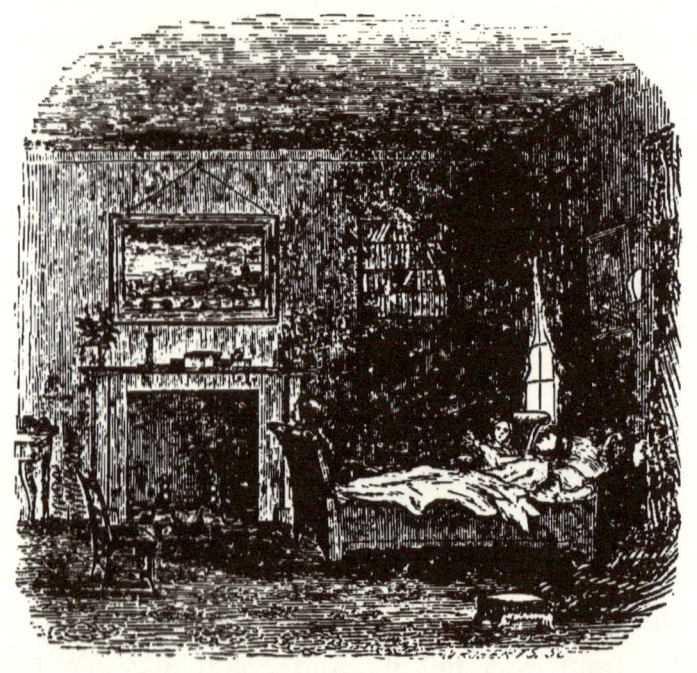

DEECHNUT'S CHAMBER.

A copy of Beechnut's picture of Paris is put into this book for a frontispiece, and the reader by referring to it from time to time, as he reads this conversation, will better understand Beech- nut's remarks, besides getting a more clear idea of some of the more important localities of the city of Paris than any mere description could possibly give.

" Yes," said Phonny, " I see it.   Which way does it run ?"

" That is a very sensible question," said Beechnut.   It is almost sensible enough to balance the folly of the observation which you made before."

" What observation ?" asked Phonny.

" The observation," replied Beechnut, " that you knew before that Paris was upon the river Seine."

" Well I *did* know it, truly," said Phonny.

" I do not doubt it," replied Beechnut.   " But there was no need of interrupting the story to boast of your knowledge."

" Well, which way *does* the Seine flow ?' asked Phonny.

" It flows toward us, as we look at the picture.   Do you see that little island in the middle of the river ?"

" Yes," said Phonny.   " I see two."

" I mean the largest," added Beechnut.

" The one nearest this way," said Phonny. " I see it."

" So do I," said Malleville.

" It is a pretty large island in reality," said Beechnut, " though it looks small in the picture. It has a great many streets and squares in it, and various public buildings and churches They call it the city."

" What for ?" asked Phonny.

" I don't know," said Beechnut. " They never call it the island, but always the city. There is a great cathedral church upon it, which is celebrated all over the world. This church has two square towers."

" Yes," said Phonny, " I see them."

" It is called the church of Notre Dame," said Beechnut. " It is not at all like the churches and meeting-houses in this country, with pews in the middle and a pulpit at one end."

" What *is* it like ?" asked Malleville.

" Oh. you can not get any idea of it," replied Beechnut, " without seeing it. The interior is of vast size, with enormous columns rising to support the arches to the roof, and when you look up it seems as if you were looking to the sky. And all around there are sculptures and monuments, all carved in stone, and great paintings on the walls, and chapels along the sides with immense numbers of little candles burning before the crucifixes and the images of the Virgin, and hundreds of persons from all parts of the world walking to and fro, and priests in white robes, chanting masses and burning in-

cense, while the sound of the organ is thundering all the time along the arches and aisles."

" I should like to go there," said Malleville.

" So should I," said Phonny, " very much indeed."

" Then besides the church," continued Beechnut, " there is an enormous hospital upon the
island, with sick people in it by the thousand.
They lie in beds placed in rows in long halls.
The nuns and nurses are walking about the
rooms taking care of these sick people, and the
physicians come round every day, bringing stu-
dents with them, and going along from bed to
bed to prescribe. The hospital is so large
that it takes a great many hours to go over
it all."

" I should not want to see so many sick people," said Malleville.

" *I* should," said Phonny.

" Can we see the hospital in the picture?"
asked Phonny.

" Not very well," replied Beechnut. " It is
not far from the church, on the right hand side
of the island."

" There are a great many bridges across the
Seine," continued Beechnut.

" Yes," said Phonny. "I mean to count

them. One, two, three, four, five, six, seven,
____:,

When Phonny had got to seven he was somewhat puzzled for the rest, as he could not count
the bridges about the island very well.

" Some of these bridges," said Beechnut, " are
wide, for carriages, and others are narrow, being intended only for foot-men. It is good fun
to go over, half-way, upon one of these bridges,
and look down upon the river."

" What do you see ?" asked Phonny.

"Oh, you see boys fishing upon the banks,'
replied Beechnut, " and a great many little boats
sailing about."

" And ships ?" asked Phonny.

" No," replied Beechnut, " you can never
have ships upon a river among bridges. The
masts are too tall."

" But they have ships in London," said Phonny, " and bridges too."

" But not together," replied Beechnut. " The
ships never go above the bridges. The bridges
are all in the upper part of the city, and the
ships in the lower. They could not have a
bridge in the lower part of the city where the
shipping is, and that is the reason that they
made the tunnel."

" I can see some of the little *boats* in the river, in the picture," said Malleville.

" Yes," said Beechnut.   " Only the river is a great deal larger in reality than it appears in the picture, and there are a great many more boats.   Then there are the great floating bathing-houses, and washing-houses, and mills."

" What are they ?" asked Phonny.

" The washing-houses," replied Beechnut, "are very long and large houses, made one story high, and handsomely painted.   They are anchored in the river, and they float upon the water.   There are rows of openings, like doors, in them, all around, opening down to the water.   At each opening there stands a woman, washing clothes in the river, and banging them when she pulls them out of the water, with a great club on the edge of the boat."

" What boat ?" asked Phonny.

" Why, the washing-house itself is a sort of monstrous boat, and there is a flat place at the edge, at the bottom of the openings, where the washer-women stand, for them to beat the clothes upon."

" Yes," said Phonny, " I understand.   But I don't see any view of the washing-houses in the picture."

"No," said Beechnut, "there is not room in such a picture for a hundredth part of what you can see in Paris itself. There are the mills besides that are not represented in the picture. They are large buildings floating upon the water with wheels at the sides of them, like the wheels of a steam-boat. The water of the river flowing by, while the boat is kept still by its moorings, makes the wheels go round, and that carries the machinery."

"How curious!" said Phonny.

"Yes," said Beechnut. "You see a great many curious things in standing upon the bridges at Paris, and looking down upon the water. Sometimes you may see something that is horrible."

"What?" asked Phonny.

"Why, you might possibly see the dead body of a man floating by. There are a great many miserable wretches in Paris, and a great many of them drown themselves in the river. Then there are others that fall in and get drowned accidentally. The police take them out as soon as they see them, but the water is always so turbid that they are not easily seen, and they float away down the river two or three miles. There, there is a great net stretched across the

BEECHNUT'S PICTURE OF PARIS. 65

The Morgue.   Uses of it.   The king's palace.

stream to catch the bodies. This net is examined every day, and all the bodies are taken
back to Paris again."

"To be buried?" asked Phonny.

"No, not immediately. They first put them
in a particular building which stands in a very
public place upon the bank of the river, where
any body can go and see them, to see if they
are their friends. This building is called the
Morgue. The bodies are put upon marble
slabs, and a little stream of water runs over
them all the time. The clothes which were
taken off from them are hung up near, for
sometimes they might be known by their
clothes."

"Can any body go in and see them?" asked
Phonny.

"Yes," said Beechnut "The door of the
Morgue is always open, and people are all the
time going in and out. I went in a great many
times."

"What did you see?" asked Phonny.

"Beechnut," said Malleville, "I wish you
would tell us about something else. I don't like
to hear so much about that."

"Well," said Beechnut, "I will. I will tell
you about the king's palace. It is that long

E

building facing this way, in the middle of the picture, with the gardens before it."

"Yes," said Phonny, "with the end to the river."

"That," continued Beechnut, "is the famous palace of the Tuilleries, where the king lives; —the king, or the emperor, or the president, whichever it is. In front of it are the gardens of the Tuilleries, full of groves of trees, and pleasant walks, and beds of beautiful flow ers."

"I can't see the flowers," said Malleville.

"No," rejoined Beechnut. "They would be too small to be seen on such a picture; but there are, in fact, a great many flowers there. Then there are beautiful marble statues, and fountains, and thousands of ladies and gentle-men walking to and fro, or sitting under the trees upon chairs kept there for the purpose, and soldiers walking about to preserve order and guard the gates."

"Won't they let any body go in," asked Phonny.

"Oh yes," replied Beechnut, "they let every body go in, provided they are neatly and prop-erly dressed, and have not any parcel in their hands. The garden is for pleasure, and they do not allow any thing that looks like business to enter there. All the world may go if they go only to enjoy themselves. At a certain hour in the evening the drum beats, and then every body must go out. The children of Paris like to go into the gardens of the Tuilleries very much. There is a great round pond of water in the middle of it, where they can sail their boats. You can see this pond in, the picture, with the fountain playing in the center of it, only it looks very small."

"Where?" said Malleville; "I don't see it."

Phonny said that he saw it, and he jumped down from his place upon the bed, went to the fire-place, and then climbing up in a chair, he pointed out the pond to Malleville.

"By-and-by," continued Beechnut, "I am going to tell you about an adventure that I had in the gardens of the Tuilleries, at this basin, or pond; but now I want you to look at the great open square, this side of the gardens of the Tuilleries, where you see two fountains, one on each side."

"Yes," said Phonny. "Here it is: and these are the fountains."

So saying, Phonny pointed at the fountains

68　　　　　Beechnut.

The obelisk.　　Ilistory of it.　　The column of the Place Vendôme.

with his finger. Then he got down from his
chair and resumed his former position upon the
bed.

"I can see them perfectly well from here,"
said he.

"There is something between those fountains," resumed Beechnut, "in the middle of
the square, which is thought very wonderful,
but I presume that it will not interest you very
much."

"What is it?" asked Phonny.

"An obelisk," replied Beechnut. "You can
see it standing up straight and tall in the middle of the square. The wonder is, that though
it is very large and very high, like a lofty steeple, it is all one single stone from top to bottom.
It was made and set up in Egypt, thousands of
years ago, and is covered with hieroglyphics.
They brought it from Egypt, and set it up in
Paris in this square. It required prodigicus
engines to move and lift such an enormous
stone."

"I see another obelisk," said Phonny.
"There it is." So saying, he pointed to a
tall column which may be seen in the picture to
the left of the gardens of the Tuilleries, rising
from a square opening among the buildings.

"No," said Beechnut, "that is not an obelisk That is the column of the Place Vendôme. There is a statue of Napoleon upon the top of it. The column is covered with brass upon the outside, from the bottom to the top, with representations of battles upon it. Napoleon got the brass by melting up between four and five hundred brass cannons that he conquered from his enemies in the wars."

"Behind the Tuilleries," continued Beechnut, "is a great parade-ground, where the troops are reviewed every morning at ten o'clock, with drums beating and colors flying."

"I should like to go and see them," said Phonny.

"So should I," said Malleville, "if they would not fire. It frightens me when they fire."

"You would like better to go to the Louvre Malleville," said Beechnut.

"Where is the Louvre?" asked Malleville.

"It is directly behind the parade-ground. It is built on four sides of a square with an open space in the center."

After attentively examining the picture for some time, Phonny and Malleville both saw the palace of the Louvre. They could easily make

out its square form, though that front of it
which was turned toward them was somewhat
concealed by smaller buildings which stood between the Louvre and the parade-ground.
Beechnut explained to them that there were
immense picture-galleries in the Louvre, consisting of long halls,—so long, some of them,
that you could scarcely see from one end to
the other,—and yet the walls were entirely covered with the most beautiful paintings, through
the whole extent. Here, he said, crowds of
ladies and gentlemen were continually walking
up and down, or sitting upon cushioned benches
and looking at the paintings, or observing the
artists who were at work everywhere along the
apartments making copies. Beechnut described
the Boulevards too, a broad and splendid street
going all around the city. The beginning of it
may be seen on the left where it commences at
a church without a steeple, seen at the corner
of the picture. This church, Beechnut said,
was a very beautiful one, and was called the
Madeleine.

Beechnut also showed Phonny and Malleville
where the great hotel was situated to which a
large proportion of the English and American
travelers who go to Paris, resort. It was on

the left of the gardens of the Tuilleries, upon the broad street which may be seen in the picture between the gardens and the columns of the Place Vendôme. The name of this hotel was the Hotel Meurice. There were pictures of carriages in the street opposite to this place, very small, so small indeed that Malleville could not very well make out what they were. Beechnut, however, told her that they were carriages, and that they were filled with English and American travelers going out to ride.

As he said this, Beechnut threw his head over upon the pillow toward the other side, so as to turn away from the picture, and exclaimed with a sigh,

"Oh, dear me! I am tired."

"But you promised to tell us the story of your adventure in the gardens of the Tuilleries,' said Phonny.

"Not now," said Beechnut. "No more now. Come to-morrow."

So Phonny got down from the bed, and perceiving that Beechnut was very tired, he took Malleville by the hand, and led her gently out of the room.

CHAPTER IV.

ARIELLE.

THE next morning, soon after breakfast, Phonny and Malleville went into Beechnut's room to ask him to tell them the story of his adventure in the gardens of the Tuilleries. They found him a great deal stronger and better than he had been the day before. He was sitting up in his bed with his back against the bolsters, and he had a pillow with a board over it, in his lap, for a table. Upon the board he had a loose pile of pictures which he had been collecting for some time from newspapers and books, with the intention of putting them into his scrap-book when he had leisure. He was now trimming the edges of these pictures with a pair of shears.

"Ah, Beechnut," said Phonny, coming up to the bedside. "You must not work. Malleville and I will trim these pictures for you."

"This is not work," replied Beechnut. "This is play."

ARIELLE. 73

Conversation.　　　The musical box.　　　Beechnut's regard for it.

"Oh no," said Phonny, "it is work to trim pictures; and hard work too to trim them straight. I have tried it. You had better let Malleville and I do it for you."

"No," said Beechnut. "I will finish the work now I have begun it, and you and Malleville may come and sit here together in the easy chair, and I will tell you the story of my adventure"

So Phonny and Malleville took their places as Beechnut had directed, and he began his story as follows.

"My father was a maker of musical boxes, and he used to live in Geneva, in Switzerland."

"Did he make your musical box for you?" asked Malleville.

Beechnut had, among his other treasures, a very handsome musical box, which played several very pretty tunes indeed. Malleville and Phonny had often taken it to hear it play. Beechnut kept it very safely in a drawer which was always very carefully locked, and he seemed to prize it very highly. Malleville knew that this musical box came with Beechnut's other valuables from France, and accordingly when she heard that Beechnut's father was a musical box-maker by trade, she thought at once that he must have made Beechnut's box.

" Yes," said Beechnut, in reply to her question ; "and it was the last box that he ever made ; and that is the reason why I value it so much."

" My father," continued Beechnut, "got along very well in making musical boxes at Geneva for some time, but at last some unlucky man invented a new way of making them by using machinery for some of the important parts, so that the boxes could be made a great deal cheaper than before."

" I should think that that was lucky," said Phonny, "not unlucky."

" It was unlucky for my father, at any rate," said Beechnut, "for he, and all other workmen like him, who only knew how to make the musi cal boxes in the old way, were thrown out of employment."

" Why did not your father learn to make them by the machinery ?" asked Phonny

" I don't know," replied Beechnut. "Perhaps he might have learned, but my mother died about that time, and that disheartened him more and more, and finally he determined to go away from Geneva. So he packed up his tools in a trunk, and sold all his furniture, and then set off with me to go to Paris."

" After he had been in Paris some time," continued Beechnut, "and could not get any thing to do, he became very much discouraged and depressed. We lived in a little room in a house upon the island that you see there in the picture ; the island that I told you was called the city."

"Was it near the church that you lived?" asked Phonny.

"No," said Beechnut, "it was at the other end of the island, the end this way. I felt very unhappy to see my father so distressed, and one day I thought I would go out and take a walk, and see if I could not find something for him to do. And if I could not do that, I thought at least that I might amuse myself by finding somebody more distressed than we were, and perhaps helping them a little in their troubles, even if we could not get out of ours.

" I walked across the bridge which leads from the city toward the Louvre. You can see it upon the picture at this end of the island. The bridge was covered with carriages and people, going and coming. When I got across the bridge, and came to the street which runs along the bank of the river, I found it full of omnibuses, coaches, and men on foot, with multitudes of people at the corners, having books and pictures for sale, and drinks of various kinds, and refreshments. There was a row of women sitting on little benches along the edge of the side-walk, exercising their various trades. One was shearing and trimming dogs, another was brushing boots for persons who were going by. A man would come up to the place and put his feet, first one and then the other, upon a little stool which she had ready for him there, while she would clean and polish his boots without having them taken off. Another had Lucifer matches to sell, another hot cakes, which she was all the time frying over a little portable furnace. Presently a *cocoa-man* came along with his cocoa-fountain on his back, and his cups tinkling."

"What does that mean?" asked Phonny.

"A cocoa-man," said Beechnut, "is a man in Paris who sells a kind of drink which they call cocoa. It is very cheap, but I don't think it is very good."

"No," said Phonny. "I have drank it, and I don't like it very well."

"It is not your kind of cocoa," rejoined

His can.　　　His tumblers.　　　The mischievous boy.

Beechnut, "that the cocoa-man sells in Paris. It is something quite different, I believe. But whatever it is, he carries it in a great flat tin can, strapped to his back, and rising high above his head. The can is gayly painted, and it has a pipe and a stop-cock, which comes out under the man's arms, so that he draws out the drink conveniently before him into little tin tumblers, which he carries in his hand. These tin tumblers he jingles together as he walks along, to let people know that the cocoa-man is coming.

"The one that came along where I was walking was stopped by a mischievous boy, who asked for two drinks of cocoa, one for himself, he said, and the other for another boy who was coming round the corner. When the cocoa-man had drawn out the drinks, the boy handed the cups back to him, asking him to hold them for a moment while he took the money out of his pocket. The cocoa-man took the cups, and while his hands were thus confined the boy turned the stop-cock and set the cocoa to running out of the can, and then ran away, laughing at the cocoa-man's distress.

THE COCOA-MAN.

" I saw it all, and went up immediately and
turned the faucet again so as to stop the running of the cocoa. The cocoa-man was very
angry with the boy, but was very thankful to
me. I lifted up the cover of his can and helped
him pour back the two cups of cocoa. He
said that he was very much obliged to me indeed, and asked me if he could not do any
thing to serve me. I told him no, unless he
could help me get something for my father to
do. He said he did not know of any thing

that he could do unless he should buy a can and become a cocoa-merchant. If my father liked that, he would teach him, he said, all about the business. Then he put his hand into his pocket and took out a *sou*, and gave it to me. He said that if he was rich, he would reward me more. I told him that I did not need any reward, but that I would take the *sou*, for it would help my father a little. So I took it, and went away."

"What is a *sou?*" asked Phonny.

"It is a piece of money like a cent," said Beechnut.

"I took my *sou*," continued Beechnut, "and walked on. Presently, as I was going across by the parade-ground, I found two small children with their *bonne*. They had been flying a small kite which their *bonne* had bought for them at a toy-shop."

"What is a *bonne?*" asked Malleville.

"Why, it is a sort of maid," replied Beech. nut, "that takes care of children, and walks out with them, and helps them play. The kite which these children had was very small, and it had a *thread* for a string. The kite had got caught in a tree, and the *bonne* could not get it down. I went to them, and offered to climb the tree

and release the kite; and I began to do so, but
a police-officer came by, and said that it was
forbidden to climb the trees. So I was obliged
to desist. The *bonne* said it was no matter.
She would pull upon the string, she said, and
perhaps the kite would come down. So she
pulled very hard, but instead of bringing the
kite down, she only broke the string off near
the kite, and then the string itself, but nothing
else, came to the ground. It was a very pretty
scarlet thread.

"The *bonne* said that I might have the thread
to pay for my kindness in trying to get the kite.
I did not know that it would be of any use to
me, but it was very pretty, and I concluded to
take it and carry it home to show to my father.
I had not any thing else to wind it on, and so I
wound it upon my *sou*, and then put it in my
pocket. Then we all went away. I went one
way, while the *bonne* and the children went another. We left the kite dangling in the tree.

"I went along into the street that you see
there in the picture, passing between the gardens of the Tuilleries and the column in the
Place Vendôme, until I came to the great iron
gate leading into the gardens. I went in.
There were thousands of ladies and gentlemen

walking about, some talking together as they walked, some looking at the fountains, or the statues, or the beds of flowers ; while there were others sitting at their leisure in chairs under the trees. I sauntered on among these crowds, not knowing where to go or what to do, until I came at length to the great circular basin which you see there in the picture, with the fountain in the middle of it. The fountain was not playing then, so that the water was smooth in every part. There were a great many people walking around the basin. There was a little boy there, rather plainly dressed, who had a small boat which he was sailing upon the water of the basin. There was a very pretty young woman with him, who, as I supposed, was nis *bonne.*"

" And was not she his *bonne?*" asked Malleville.

" No," replied Beechnut. " I found out afterward that she was his sister, though I did not know it at the time. He called her Arielle."

" What a pretty name," said Malleville.

" And what was the boy's name ?" asked Phonny.

" Adolphe," said Beechnut.

" That is not a very pretty name," said Phonny.

F

" No," added Beechnut, " but it was a very pretty boy, and he had a very pretty boat. His sister had rigged it for him, and he had come out to sail it that day for the first time. He had a string tied to the bows of the boat to keep it from getting away from him, but just as I came up to the place, he had, in some way or other accidentally dropped his string, and the boat was sailing away over the water out of his reach There were some other boys there who began to laugh at him, and went about to pick up little pebble-stones to throw at the boat and make it go away farther. Poor Adolphe was greatly distressed and began to cry. Arielle looked distressed too. She begged Adolphe not to cry, and said that she would contrive some way or other to get his boat back again. But when she looked at it and saw it floating slowly away, farther and farther, she did not know what to do."

" Hoh !" said Phonny. " Why did not the boy pull up his trowsers and go right in and get it ?"

" The police would not have allowed h m to do that," replied Beechnut. " The police are very strict about all such things as that, in the public gardens in Paris. Besides, I presum the water was too deep."

" I immediately recollected my long thread," continued Beechnut, " and thought that I could get back the boat in some way or other by means of that. So I went up to the brink of the basin and said to the other boys, don't let us throw stones at the poor little fellow's vessel. Let us try to get it back for him.

" They then stopped throwing stones, but they said that there was no way to get the vessel back. One of the boys had a small pebble-stone in his hand which he had not yet thrown. I asked him to let me look at it. I then took out my scarlet thread, and asked him if he thought it would be possible to tie that thread to the pebble-stone so as to make it hold. He said he thought it would ; and then I asked him to try and see if he could do it."

" Why did not you do it yourself?" asked Phonny.

" Because," replied Beechnut, " I wanted to get those boys interested in bringing back the vessel, by giving them something to do about it."

" That was a good plan," said Phonny.

" Yes," said Beechnut. " If I had gone for. ward by myself alone to get back the vessel, es· pecially after having reproved them for throwing stones at it, I should perhaps have had their

ill-will, and when I had got the boat pretty near
the shore, they might possibly have pushed it
out again.   But I knew that if I engaged them
to help me, they would be as much interested in
getting back the vessel as i."

"And did you get it back?" asked Malleville.

"I will tell you," replied Beechnut.   "The
boy tied the end of my scarlet thread to the
pebble-stone as carefully as he could, and then
I unwound a considerable length of the thread
from the *sou*, and placed it in a little coil upon
the brink of the basin.   I then asked one of the
other boys, the largest one in the company,
whether he thought he could toss the stone
gently over the vessel into the water beyond it,
in such a manner that the line should fall across
the deck of it.   'Oh, yes,' he said, 'easily
enough.' "

"Immediately," continued Beechnut, "seve
ral of the other boys wanted the privilege of
throwing the stone; but I told them we would
take turns in doing it, for as the vessel had
floated away so far from the shore, it was not
at all probable, I said, that the operation would
succeed on the first trial.   Indeed, I hoped that
it would not, for I wished to give several of the

boys an opportunity to toss the stone. And in fact it did not succeed the first time. They had to try three times. The third time the stone went into the water a little way beyond the vessel, and the thread fell down upon the deck between the two masts. 'Now,' said I, 'gently, boys, gently. Pull slow and very steadily.'

"The boys began to pull upon the thread, and they drew the stone up until it came against the farthest side of the vessel, and then, by drawing in very gently and steadily, the vessel was brought in slowly toward the shore. As soon as it came within reach I took it out, released the thread and the pebble from it, and gave it to Adolphe. He seized it eagerly and ran off as fast as he could go, saying, 'come, Arielle! come!'

"Arielle, however, remained behind to thank me and the other boys for getting the vessel, and while we were talking about it, Adolphe came slowly back again, with his vessel in his hand. The boys in reply to Arielle's thanks said, that she was not under any obligation to them at all. Getting back the vessel, they said, was good fun, and they wanted Adolphe to put it into the water again, and let them push it off, in order to

give some of the other boys an opportunity to
toss the stone and get it back. But Adolphe
was not willing to do this, and he was so afraid
that in some way or other his vessel would get
put into the water again, that he was very impatient to go away. He pulled Arielle so hard
by the arm while she was talking with me, that
she began to walk slowly along, and as Arielle
was speaking to me at the time I walked along
with her. Thus we all went on together up the
grand alley, toward the palace of the Tuilleries.
You can see where we went upon the picture."

"Stop," said Phonny. "Wait till I look and
see."

So saying, Phonny went to the fire-place and
climbed up into a chair before the picture, and
then helped Malleville up and let her stand by
his' side. The representation of the place was
so small upon the picture that the children could
not see very well. Still they could make out
the basin, and the grand alley leading toward
the palace.

"As we walked along, Arielle said that she
was very much obliged to me indeed, more to me,
she said, than to all the other boys put together ;
for it was owing to me entirely that the boat
was recovered. She said that she lived in a cer-

tain street not far from the Boulevards, and that her father was a lithographic printer, and that her business was to color the prints when they were engraved. She said also that if I would go with her to her rooms, she would give me one of her pictures, and let me see how she colored them ; and she asked me if there was not any thing else that she could do for me.

" I told her that I should like very much indeed to see her color her pictures, but that what I wanted most was something for my father to do. She asked me what my father *could* do, and what sort of a place he wanted to get. I told her as much as I knew about him, and then she said that they wanted to get a porter at the house where she lived, and that perhaps he would like that situation. He would have a fine opportunity, she said, to make musical-boxes in the porter's lodge."

"I don't know what a porter is," said Malleville, "or a porter's lodge."

"There are different kinds of porters," said Beechnut. "In this country, he is a man who carries trunks about. But the kind of porter that Arielle meant was not that. It is a different business altogether. The porter that she meant, has a small room at the entrance of a

88 BEECHNUT.

Plan of the great houses in Paris.   The *concierge*.

great house to attend to the people that go in and out. The houses in Paris are very large. Some of them are built around an open court, and have ranges of apartments for a great many different families. There is a great door in the middle of the front of the house, large enough sometimes for carriages to drive in. At the entrance of these houses there is a little room, or an office, with a sort of window opening out into the passage-way, where the porter sits all the time to keep the door, and see who goes out and in, and to answer questions about the people that live there, and take letters for them. and let them in at night after the doors have been locked, and to do all such things."

"I don't see how he can do all those things," said Phonny, "and stay all the time in his own little room."

"Why, which of those things is there," asked Beechnut, "that he could not do in his room?"

"He could not open the door," replied Phonny, "and let people in."

"As to that," replied Beechnut, "the front door is always left open all day, so that people can come in themselves."

"Then what prevents the thieves and robbers from getting in?" asked Phonny.

" The porter himself," replied Beechnut, "who sits in his little office where he can see every body that goes in and out. Thus, you see, that in the day-time there is no going to the door to let people in. If the persons that come belong to the house, they come directly in, and passing by the porter's lodge, they go directly to their own apartments. If they are strangers or visitors, they come in too, as far as to the porter's lodge, and there stop and tell what they want."

"But then," continued Beechnut, "at night, after the house is locked up, if any body comes, the porter has to open the door and let them in, though he does this without going out of his own room."

" How does he do it ?" asked Phonny.

" There is a cord," answered Beechnut, "that hangs near his window, which is con nected with wires along the walls, and the last wire is fastened to the night-latch, so that by pulling the cord the door is unfastened, and the person let in. I have got up and pulled the cord for my father in the night a great many times."

" And did your father get the porter's place at that house ?" asked Phonny.

"Yes," replied Beechnut. "I went home and told him what Arielle had said, and he went directly to the house and applied for the place. I went with him. My father showed the proprietor his recommendations, and the proprietor engaged him. We lived in that porter's lodge two or three years."

"And did Arielle live in that same house?" asked Malleville.

"Yes," said Beechnut. "She had a room very high up indeed, but it was very pleasant when we once got there. Her room was very neatly arranged, and she used to sit at a table by a window all the morning, coloring pictures for the print-sellers in the Boulevards. She colored them beautifully. When she had no pictures to color, she used to draw pictures on stone for her father to print. It was she who first taught me to draw, and, at last, when I came away, she gave me that picture of Paris. My father made my musical box too in the porter's lodge, at his leisure time. It was the last musical box that he ever made."

Here there was a long pause. Beechnut was thinking of his father, and of the happy times he used to have in going up to see Arielle in her room, and in sitting with his father in the porter's lodge, and seeing the people that were incessantly coming and going. Phonny and Malleville were thinking of the story that they had heard.

Beechnut, after remaining silent for a short time, took the board, with all his cuttings upon it, and put it away at the foot of the bed. He then laid his head down upon the pillow, telling the children that some other day he would tell them more, but that now they might go away.

"Well, come, Malleville," said Phonny.

So they got down out of the easy chair, and went away.

CHAPTER V.

PREPARING FOR A RIDE.

BEECHNUT was so patient and submissive during his confinement to his room on account of his wound, and obeyed so implicitly all the orders and directions both of the physician and the nurse, that he recovered very rapidly. At last, he advanced so far that he could sit up in the easy-chair, with his foot upon a cushioned stool before him. Here he amused himself one afternoon in making a pair of crutches, and the next day he walked upon his crutches all about the room. Phonny was so much pleased with this operation, that he said he wished that Beechnut would make *him* a pair of crutches. Those which Beechnut had made for himself were too long for Phonny, though he tried a long time to walk upon them.

"Won't you make *me* some crutches?" asked Phonny.

"Yes," said Beechnut, "the first time that you get hurt, so that you can not walk upon your legs."

"No," said Phonny, "I want them now. Or stay, I'll hurt myself now, and then I *must* have them."

So saying, he tumbled down upon the floor, and pretended to have sprained his ankle dreadfully; and then he went limping about the room, moaning piteously, and making the most ludicrous contortions, both of face and figure, greatly to Malleville's amusement.

"I can't make you any crutches," said Beechnut, "but I will make you a pair of stilts some time, if you will go and get leave for me to take a ride."

"Who shall I get to give you the leave?" asked Phonny.

"Any body," replied Beechnut, "who has authority to give it. Your mother, or the doctor, or the nurse."

"The nurse has gone home," said Phonny. "I'll go and ask mother."

Phonny went out, and it was more than an hour before he returned. He came at last running into the room, and calling out in great glee that he had got permission. He had gone to his mother first, and she had said that she could not take the responsibility of giving Beechnut leave to ride, but that Phonny must

94 BEECHNUT.

Phonny goes to see the doctor.   Leave to take a ride.

go to the doctor. So Phonny immediately set off to find the doctor, who lived about half a mile from Mrs. Henry's. Phonny found him at home, very fortunately, and after hearing Phonny's request, he said that on the whole he thought it would be safe for Beechnut to take a ride, if he would put his foot upon a good pile of cushions, and not drive faster than a walk.

"But then there is one difficulty," said Phonny, "there is nobody to harness the horse."

"Where are the men?" asked Beechnut.

"They have both gone off into the woods," said Phonny. "But I can go and find them, and get one of them to come home."

"No," said Beechnut. "You and I can harness the horse. That is, we *could*, if it were not for one difficulty."

"What is that?" asked Phonny.

"You will not be willing to follow my directions," said Beechnut.

"Yes, I will," replied Phonny. "I will follow them exactly."

"Very well," said Beechnut, "we will try it. In the first place, then, you and Malleville may go down and see if you can open the wagon-house doors, and if you can, then try to run the wagon out. *You* must take hold of the shafts, and Malleville must push behind. In this way get the wagon along as far as you can toward the back door."

Phonny and Malleville succeeded in performing this part of the operation very well. They got the doors open and backed the wagon out, and then they succeeded, though not without a great deal of tugging and pushing, in getting it along near to the back door. Phonny then came up into Beechnut's room again for further orders.

"Now," said Beechnut, "which will be the best horse for us to take?"

"The Marshall," said Phonny.

"Well," said Beechnut, "you may take the Marshall. Go to his stall, and unfasten him and lead him out. You need not trouble yourself about keeping out of the way of his fore-feet, for all you have got to do if he treads on you is to tickle him a little under his shoulder, and he will take his foot off."

Beechnut said this with so grave an air that Phonny thought he was in earnest, so he replied soberly,

"Yes, and in the mean time I should be dreadfully hurt."

"Never mind that," said Beechnut. "You could tickle yourself then, perhaps, and that would relieve the pain."

"No," said Phonny, positively. "I shall not do any such thing."

"Just as you please," said Beechnut. "If you think it is best not to get trod upon at all, I have no objection. When you have got the Marshall out of the yard, lead him into the carriage-house and fasten him by the halter to one of the pins. Then see if you can put the harness upon his back. You may arrange the harness if you can, properly upon his back, but do not attempt to put the crupper on. I will attend to that when you bring the horse to the door. Do you think that you can put the *collar* on?"

"Yes," said Phonny, "easily enough."

"Well," said Beechnut, "if you can, you may, and then lead the horse to the door and fasten him at the post. When you have done that, come and tell me."

So Phonny went away to execute his commission. He found no difficulty in untying the Marshall, and leading him out of the stable. Of course after what Beechnut had said, he took special care not to stand in the way of the Marshall's feet. He led the horse into the carriage-house, and fastened him to one of the great wooden pins driven into the beams to hang the harnesses upon. Then he took down the wagon-harness and put it upon the horse's back. He got it on first wrong side before, and in chang-ing it he got it twisted. It took him some time to get it right. He, however, succeeded at last, and then he put the collar on. Malleville stood by all the time looking on. He also succeeded in putting on the bridle, the horse aiding him in the operation by holding down his head and opening his mouth for the bits.

" I have a great mind to put the crupper on," said Phonny, " and then it will be all done."

" No," said Malleville. " Beechnut said that you must not try to put the crupper on."

" That," said Phonny, " was only because he supposed that I could not do it. But I can: and he will be very glad to find that it is done. I can do it as well as not by standing up upon this bench."

The bench which Phonny referred to was one which was standing in the carriage-house near one corner, and Phonny, after bringing it out into the middle of the floor, led the horse up to the side of it, in such a position, that he thought

G

when standing upon the bench he could put the crupper on. When he had brought up the horse into the right position, he asked Malleville to hold him by the halter, while he got up upon the bench. The horse's head was turned away from the door.

Malleville could hold the Marshall's head very easily by his halter, but, unfortunately, she could not hold his body, and the horse, perhaps suspecting what Phonny was going to do, stepped round a little to one side, while Phonny was getting up upon the bench, so as to move away just far enough from the bench to prevent Phonny from reaching him.

" There !" said Phonny, " now he has moved away. What did he do that for ?"

So Phonny got down from the bench again, and turning the horse entirely round, he brought him up to the bench again, nearer than before.

" There," said he, " keep him exactly so, Malleville."

Malleville took the bridle and held it as nearly as possible in the exact position in which Phonny put it into her hand. She found, however, that holding the bridle was not holding the horse, for just as Phonny stepped up upon the bench again, to make a new attempt to put on

the crupper, the horse stepped away as before.
It was only a very little that he moved--very
little indeed ; but it was enough effectually to
prevent Phonny from reaching him.

" There !" said Phonny, a little impatiently.
" Now you have let him move away."

" Why, I could not help it," said Malleville.
" I held him exactly as you told me."

" Then I wish you would go round by his side,"
said Phonny, "and push him back into his place."

On hearing this direction, Malleville dropped
the bridle and went along toward the Marshall's
side, intending to push him back toward the
bench again, according to Phonny's suggestion.
But the horse, finding himself at liberty, and
seeing the door of the carriage-house open before him,—for in turning him round to bring
him up to the bench the second time, Phonny
had given him a position with his head toward
the door—quietly walked off out into the yard.
He went first to the well to see if there was any
water in the tub where he usually drank, but
finding that there was not any, he moved away
to one side where the grass was very green and
beautiful, and began to crop and eat it ; though
the bits, which were in his mouth, were very
much in his way.

Phonny, after uttering some exclamations of disappointment and chagrin, followed the horse and attempted to catch him. But he could not do it. Whenever he got near to him, the Marshall would shake his head and walk away.

"Oh, dear me !" said Phonny. "Now what shall I do? He won't be caught."

"You must go and tell Beechnut," said Malleville.

"No," said Phonny, "that will not do any good. Beechnut can not catch him,—with nothing but one foot and his crutches."

The truth was, Phonny was ashamed to go to Beechnut and tell him of the difficulty, since he had got into it by disobeying his instructions. He made, accordingly, several more attempts to catch the horse, but in vain. He began to be in great perplexity, and his distress was finally much increased by hearing the thumping of he crutches upon the stairs, which warned him .hat Beechnut was coming down.

To Phonny's great relief, Beechnut did not seem at all surprised to see the horse astray, when he appeared at the door. On the contrary, he sat down upon the step quite at his ease, and laid the crutches down by his side.

"Phonny!" said Beechnut, at length, when he was comfortably seated.

"What?" said Phonny.

"Come here," said Beechnut.

So Phonny came.

"Go into the house and bring me out a handful of coarse salt," said Beechnut.

"Yes," said Phonny, "I will." And so saying, he ran off eagerly into the house, very glad to escape from the presence of Beechnut, without having incurred his displeasure. He expected that Beechnut would have appeared displeased, but he did not. Beechnut looked and spoke as placidly as usual, just as if nothing had happened.

In a few minutes Phonny returned with the salt.

Beechnut took the salt in his hand, and then creeping down to the lowermost step of the door, which was formed of a great flat stone, he held it out toward the horse.

"Now," said he to Phonny, "do you and Malleville go and drive the Marshall up this way. Drive him very gently."

So Phonny and Malleville, each taking up a little stick from the ground, went round to the farther side of the Marshall, and began driv ing him toward Beechnut. The horse moved slowly along, cropping the grass by the way, until he came near to the door, Beechnut calling him all the time by his name.

CATCHING THE HORSE.

As soon as the horse saw the salt in Beechnut's hand, he advanced at once toward it. Beechnut poured it out upon the stone, and the horse immediately began to lap it up with his tongue.

"Now!" said Phonny, "catch hold of the bridle, Beechnut; quick!"

"There's no haste," said Beechnut. "Let him finish eating his salt."

The horse, after lapping up all the salt from the stone until the spot where it had been laid was perfectly clean, looked up at Beechnut for more.

Beechnut quietly put forth his hand and took hold of the Marshall's bridle.

"This is not cheating you, old fellow," said Beechnut, looking the horse in the face. "I would not cheat such an honest old soldier as you are for the world. It is a bargain that I make with you. I give you an ounce and a half of salt, and you allow yourself to be caught peaceably, so as to go and take me to ride. It is a regular bargain; and if you are not entirely satisfied with the consideration, I will give you another ounce and a half of salt when we come back."

The Marshall said nothing, but turned his head round very deliberately and looked at the wagon.

"Yes," said Beechnut, "we are going to take the wagon, I know, and Phonny and Malleville in it, besides myself; and that, I admit, makes rather a heavy load. But then we are going to let you walk all the way. The doctor says that we must not go faster than a walk. Think of that. You are going to walk all the way, whether it is up hill, down hill, or level. Think of that."

The horse turned his head round again and looked toward Beechnut.

"He agrees to it," said Beechnut. "So come, Phonny, and lead him to the wagon."

Malleville then, at Beechnut's direction, lifted the shafts of the wagon and held them up, while Phonny backed the horse in between them. Phonny then took hold of the leather loops which hung down from the saddle on each side, and passed them over the ends of the shafts, doing this first on one side of the horse, and then going round and doing it on the other. The shafts were thus held up.

"*Now*, Phonny," said Beechnut, "you may see if you can put on the crupper. The shafts will keep the horse still in his place. You can get a chair in the kitchen to stand upon."

Phonny went into the kitchen and got a chair, and though he found the operation a very diffi- cult one, he succeeded in putting on the crup- per. Then slipping the harness-saddle for- ward into its place, he buckled the girth, and proceeded to complete the harnessing.

"I suppose," said Beechnut, while Phonny was engaged in these operations, "that the way in which the Marshall got away from you in the carriage-house was, that you were trying to crupper him.'

"Yes," said Phonny, looking a little ashamed. "But how did you know?"

"Why, I supposed that you would try to crupper him, of course. You know I told you that you would not obey the directions. That is the nature of boys. They feel so self-sufficient and so self-confident, and are so eager to show what they can do, that they always spoil all by undertaking too much."

Phonny went on buckling the straps, but did not answer.

"One day," continued Beechnut, "I set a boy at work wheeling wood, and I charged him very particularly to load light, so that he could run his loads along safely and easily. Instead of that, he piled up his very first load so high that he could not wheel it at all, or even steady it. He had not taken three steps before the load upset and broke the wheel-barrow."

The boy that Beechnut referred to in this illustration was Phonny himself.

"Another time," continued Beechnut, "I

gave a boy some work to do in cleaning away the stones from a path. There were a great many small stones lying loosely upon the ground, which he might easily have handled. But instead of taking those, he selected one which was firmly embedded in the ground, so as to show a small part of it above the surface of the path, and went into the barn and brought out a crow-bar to pry it up with. After trying for some time in vain, he threw down the bar, and came in and told me that the stones in the path were so heavy that he could not lift them."

This was Phonny too.

Malleville laughed very heartily at this story, not knowing that Phonny himself was the person that Beechnut referred to.

" Who was the boy, Beechnut?" said she. " What was his name?"

" His name?" rejoined Beechnut. " His name, I think, ought to have been Folly, but I believe it was in fact spelled with a double n instead of a double l.

Malleville could not understand what Beech-nut meant by that, and while she was perplexing herself in vain to comprehend it, Beechnut asked her to go 'nto the house and get two sofa

cushions. Phonny had by this time finished
the harnessing, and Beechnut then sent him
into the barn to get a large armful of hay.
When the hay was brought, Phonny and Beechnut took the seat out of the wagon, and put the
hay in its place, covering the bottom of the
wagon with it entirely. Phonny then got the
great bear-skin and spread it down over the
hay, and the sofa cushions which Malleville had
brought out in the mean time, were also put in.
Beechnut then climbed into the wagon from behind, and placing the sofa cushions one upon
the other in the back part of the wagon upon
the bear-skin, he lay down at full length, with
his head and shoulders upon the cushions.
Phonny and Malleville then climbed in and
took seats upon the bear-skin, one on each side
of Beechnut.

"You must drive, Phonny," said Beechnut.

So Phonny took the reins, and chirruping to
the horse, as a signal that he was to go on, he
guided him out through the great gate, and
turned him down the road.

"Stop one moment," said Beechnut.

So Phonny reined in the horse, and asked
what was the matter.

"Don't you think," said Beechnut, "that you

would enjoy your ride more if you were first to be punished for disobeying me, in harnessing the horse ?"

" I don't know," said Phonny, thoughtfully.

" I think you would," said Beechnut. " When you are once punished, it will be all over and settled."

" Well," said Phonny, " what shall the punishment be ?"

" How would it do," rejoined Beechnut, " for you to get out and *walk*, say for a quarter of a mile ?"

" Then who shall drive ?" asked Phonny.

" Malleville," replied Beechnut.

" Yes," said Malleville, " that will be a good punishment."

" Or," continued Beechnut, "you might remain in the wagon and not be allowed to drive at all for the whole ride. Let Malleville drive all the way."

" Yes," said Malleville. '" I like that."

" There is one objection to both these punisn-ments," added Beechnut, "and that is, that there is no disgrace in them. There ought to be some disgrace in a punishment. How would it do for me to tie your hands behind you and then tumble you in the back part of the wagon,

PREPARING FOR A RIDE.

for a culprit; and let you lie there for a quarter of a mile, instead of walking."

Phonny was much amused at this proposal, and said that he should like such a punishment very well.

" Or else," continued Beechnut, " make you mount upon the horse, with your face toward his tail, and ride in that way for a quarter of a mile. I have heard that that is a kind of punishment that is adopted in some countries, in the case of very great offenders."

" Yes," said Phonny, clapping his hands, " I should like that best of all."

" I think that will be best," said Beechnut. " It is particularly appropriate on this account, that while in that position, you will have the crupper directly before you, in full view, as a perpetual memorial of your offence."

It was thus finally determined that riding backward should be Phonny's punishment. He, accordingly, passed the reins into Malleville's hands, and then climbing up upon the horse by means of the shafts, he took his seat as well as he could upon the top of the harness, with his back to the horse's head. Both he himself and Malleville were greatly amused during the operation. His seat was very uncomfortable, but

Beechnut said that that made it all the better for punishment. There was some difficulty for a time, in respect to the reins, but Phonny finally placed them one on each side of him, as he sat upon the horse, and then made a ring with his thumb and finger on each side to pass them through.

After riding so for about a quarter of a mile, Beechnut told him that his punishment was over, and allowed him to get into the wagon again.

The whole party then rode on together, the horse walking slowly along, quite at his ease, and wondering what new notion Beechnut had taken, which led him to drive so slow.

CHAPTER VI.

EMBELLISHMENT.

WHEN Phonny and Malleville found themselves riding quietly along in the wagon in Beechnut's company, the first thought which occurred to them, after the interest and excitement awakened by the setting out had passed in some measure away was, that they would ask him to tell them a story. This was a request which they almost always made in similar circumstances. In all their rides and rambles, Beechnut's stories were an unfailing resource, furnishing them with an inexhaustible fund, of amusement sometimes, and sometimes of instruction.

"Well," said Beechnut, in answer to their request, "I will tell you now about my voyage across the Atlantic ocean."

"Yes," exclaimed Malleville, "I should like to hear about that very much indeed."

"Shall I tell the story to you just as it was.'

asked Beechnut,—"as a sober matter of fact? or shall I embellish it a little?"

"I don't know what you mean by embellishing it?" said Malleville.

"Why, not telling exactly what is true," said Beechnut, "but inventing something to add to it, to make it interesting."

"I want to have it true," said Malleville, "and interesting too."

"But sometimes," replied Beechnut, "interesting things don't happen; and in such cases, if we should only relate what actually does happen, the story would be likely to be dull."

"I think you had better embellish the story a little," said Phonny. "Just a *little*, you know."

"I don't think I can do that very well," replied Beechnut. "If I attempt to relate the actual facts, I depend simply on my memory, and I can confine myself to what my memory teaches; but if I undertake to follow my invention, I must go wherever it leads me."

"Well," said Phonny, "I think you had better embellish the story at any rate; for I want it to be interesting."

"So do I," said Malleville.

"Then," said Beechnut, "I will give you an

embellished account of my voyage across the Atlantic.

"But, in the first place, I must tell you how it happened that my father decided to leave Paris and come to America. It was mainly on my account. My father was well enough con-tented with his situation, so far as he himself was concerned, and he was able to save a large part of his salary, so as to lay up a considerable sum of money every year. But he was anx-ious about me.

"There seemed to be nothing," continued Beechnut, "for me to do, and nothing desirable for me to look forward to, when I should be come a man."

"Why could not you color pictures," asked Phonny, "like Arielle?"

"I did learn to color pictures," replied Beechnut, "and I might, I suppose, after a time, have got good employment in doing that. But my father thought that it was not very healthy work, to be confined in a sitting posture so long. Then, besides, if I should begin life by coloring pictures, I should have to go on color-ing pictures all my days. Every thing is so exactly regulated in that country, that there is very little opportunity to rise in the world

II

there.   Almost every body must go on to the
end of his life just as he begins it.

"My father thought, therefore, that though
it would perhaps be better for *him* to remain in
France, it would probably be better for *me*, if
he should come to America, where he said people might rise in the world according to their
talents, thrift, and industry.   He was sure, he
said, that I should rise, for, you must understand, he considered me an extraordinary boy."

"Well," said Phonny, "*I* think you are an
extraordinary boy."

"Yes, but my father thought," rejoined
Beechnut, "that I was something very extraordinary indeed.   He thought I was a genius."

"So do I," said Phonny.

"He used to tell Arielle and her father so,"
continued Beechnut, "and he said he thought it
would in the end be a great deal better for him
to come to America, where I might become a
man of some consequence in the world; and
he said that he should enjoy his own old age a
great deal better, even in a strange land, if he
could see me going on prosperously in life, than
to remain all his days in that porter's lodge,
while I was coloring pictures in the attic.

"And yet we used to have very pleasant

times in the porter's lodge. We had a great many good suppers there together,—Arielle and her father and brother, and my father and I. Sometimes *they* would come down and have supper with us, and at other times we would go and sup with them. We used to call these entertainments *dinners*, though they were in the evening. People do not dine in Paris till the day is over. After the dinner or supper, whichever it was, our fathers would sit and talk, drinking coffee, and we children would play. Arielle would help us draw pictures and make boats. What fine grapes we used to have to eat in those days!

"However, notwithstanding that it was so pleasant there, father thought that it would be best for him and me to come to America; and Arielle's father said, that if, after we reached this country, we sent back a favorable report, he would come too, and bring Arielle and Adolphe."

" That would be good," said Phonny.

" But I am forgetting," said Beechnut. " I promised to embellish the story, and I am only telling you the plain and sober matters of fact."

"But it is interesting," said Malleville. "I like to hear about Arielle and the pictures."

"Yes," said Beechnut, "Arielle was a very excellent girl. I liked her very much indeed. She took a great deal of pains to color that picture of Paris for me, and after it was ready, she rolled it up very carefully upon a round stick—or *bâton*, as she called it,—and then packed it safely in my chest. I had a chest to carry my things in, and my father had two chests, one for his tools and instruments, and the other for his clothes and other articles. He had, besides, a common-sized trunk for such things as he and I would want in the course of the voyage. All the money that he had saved he got changed into gold, at an office in the Boulevards : but then he was very much perplexed to decide how it was best to carry it."

"Why did not he pack it up in his chest?" asked Phonny.

"He was afraid," replied Beechnut, "that his chest might be broken open, or unlocked by false keys, on the voyage, and that the money might be thus stolen away. So he thought that he would try to hide it somewhere, in some small thing that he could keep with him all the voyage."

"Could not he keep his chest with him all the voyage?" asked Phonny.

" No," said Beechnut. " The chests and all large parcels of baggage, belonging to the passengers, must be sent down into the hold of the ship out of the way. It is only a very little baggage that the people are allowed to keep with them between the decks. My father wished very much to keep his gold with him, and yet he was afraid to keep it in a bag, or in any other similar package, in his little trunk, for then whoever saw it would know that it was gold, and so, perhaps, form some plan to rob him of it.

"While we were considering what plan it would be best to adopt for the gold, Arielle proposed to hide it in my *top*. I had a very large top which my father had made for me. It was painted yellow outside, with four stripes of bright blue passing down over it from the stem to the point. When the top was in motion, both the yellow ground and the blue stripes entirely disappeared, and the top appeared to be of a uniform green color. Then when it came to its rest again, the original colors would reappear."

"How curious!" said Malleville. "Why would it do so?"

"Why, when it was revolving," said Beechnut, "the yellow and the blue were blended together in the eye, and that made green. Yellow and blue always make green. Arielle colored my top, after my father had made it, and then my father varnished it, over the colors, and that fixed them.

"This top of mine was a monstrous large one, and being hollow, Arielle thought that the gold could all be put inside. She said she thought that that would be a very safe hiding-place too, since nobody would think of looking into a top for gold. But my father said that he thought that the space would not be quite large enough, and then if any body should happen to see the top, and should touch it, the weight of it would immediately reveal the secret.

"At last my father thought of a plan which he believed would answer the purpose very per-fectly. We had a very curious old clock. It was made by my grandfather, who was a clock-maker in Geneva. There was a little door in the face of the clock, and whenever the time came for striking the hours, this door would open, and a little platform would come out with a tree upon it. There was a beautiful little bird upon the tree, and when the clock had done striking, the bird would flap its wings and sing. Then the platform would slide back into its place, the door would shut, and the clock go on ticking quietly for another hour.

" This clock was made to go," continued Beechnut, " as all other clocks are, by two heavy weights, which were hung to the wheel-work by strong cords. The cords were wound round some of the wheels, and as they slowly descended by their weight, they made the wheels go round. There was a contrivance inside the clock to make the wheels go slowly and regularly, and not spin round too fast, as they would have done if the weights had been left to themselves. This is the way that clocks are always made.

" Now, my father," continued Beechnut, " had intended to take this old family clock with him to America, and he now conceived the idea of hiding his treasure in the weights. The weights were formed of two round tin canisters filled with something very heavy. My father said he did not know whether it was shot or sand. He unsoldered the bottom from these canisters, and found that the filling was shot. He poured out the shot, put his gold pieces in, in place of it, and then filled up all the interstices between and around the gold pieces, with sand, to prevent the money from jingling. Then he soldered the bottom of the canisters on again,

and no one would have known that the weights
were any thing more than ordinary clock weights.
He then packed the clock in a box and put the box
in his trunk. It did not take up a great deal of
room, for he did not take the case of the clock,
but only the face and the works, and the two
weights, which last he packed carefully and se-
curely in the box, one on each side of the clock
itself.

"When we got to Havre, all our baggage was
examined at the custom-house, and the officers
allowed it all to pass. When they came to the
clock, my father showed them the little door
and the bird inside, and they said that it was
very curious. They did not pay any attention
to the weights at all.

"When we went on board of the vessel, our
chests were put by the side of an immense heap
of baggage, upon the deck, where some seamen
were at work lowering it down into the hold,
through a square opening in the deck of the ship.
As for the trunk, my father took that with him
to the place where he was going to be, himself,
during the voyage. This place was called the
steerage. It was crowded full of men, women,
and children, all going to America. Some
talked French, some German, some Dutch, and

there were ever so many babies that were too little to talk at all. Pretty soon the vessel sailed.

"We did not meet with any thing remarkable on the voyage, except that once we saw an iceberg."

"What is that?" asked Malleville.

"It is a great mountain of ice," replied Beechnut, "floating about in the sea on the top of the water. I don't know how it comes to be there."

"I should not think it would float upon the top of the water," said Phonny. "All the ice that I ever saw in the water, sinks into it."

"It does not sink to the bottom," said Malleville.

"No," replied Phonny; "but it sinks down until the top of the ice is just level with the water. But Beechnut says that his iceberg rose up like a mountain."

"Yes," said Beechnut, "it was several hundred feet high above the water, all glittering in the sun. And I think that if you look at any small piece of ice floating in the water, you will see that a small part of it rises above the surface."

"Yes," said Phonny, "a very little."

"It is a certain proportion of the whole mass," rejoined Beechnut. "They told us on board our vessel that about one tenth part of the iceberg was above the water, the rest, that is, nine tenths, was under it. So you see what an enormous big piece of ice it must have been, to have only one tenth part of it tower up so high.

"There was one thing very curious and beautiful about our iceberg," said Beechnut. "We came in sight of it one day about sunset, just after a shower. The cloud, which was very large and black, had passed off into the west, and there was a splendid rainbow upon it. It happened, too, that when we were nearest to the iceberg, it lay toward the west, and, of course, toward the cloud, and it ap-peared directly under the rainbow, and the iceberg and the rainbow made a most magnificent spectacle. The iceberg, which was very bright and dazzling in the evening sun, looked like an enormous diamond, with the rainbow for the setting."

"How curious," said Phonny.

"Yes," said Beechnut, "and to make it more remarkable still, a whale just then came along

directly before the iceberg, and spouted there
two or three times; and as the sun shone very
brilliantly upon the jet of water which the
whale threw into the air, it made a sort of
silver rainbow below, in the center of the
picture."

"How beautiful it must have been!" said
Phonny.

"Yes," rejoined Beechnut, "very beautiful
indeed. We saw a great many beautiful spec-
tacles on the sea; but then, on the other hand,
we saw some that were dreadful."

"Did you?" asked Phonny. "What?"

"Why, we had a terrible storm and shipwreck at the end," said Beechnut. "For three
days and three nights the wind blew almost a
hurricane. They took in all the sails, and let
the ship drive before the gale under bare poles.
She went on over the seas for five hundred
miles, howling all the way like a frightened dog."

"Were you frightened?" asked Phonny.

"Yes," said Beechnut. "When the storm
first came on, several of the passengers came
up the hatchways, and got upon the deck to see
it; and then we could not get down again, for
the ship gave a sudden pitch just after we came
up, and knocked away the step-ladder. We

were terribly frightened. The seas were break-
ing over the forecastle and sweeping along the
decks, and the shouts and outcries of the captain and the sailors made a dreadful din. At
last, they put the step-ladder in its place again,
and we got down. Then they put the hatches
on, and we could not come out any more."

"The hatches," said Phonny, "what are
they ?'

"The hatches," replied Beechnut, "are a sort
of scuttle-doors that cover over the square
openings in the deck of a ship. They always
have to put them on and fasten them down in
a great storm."

Just at this time the party happened to ar-
rive at a place where two roads met, and as
there was a broad and level space of ground
at the junction, where it would be easy to turn
the wagon, Beechnut said that he thought it
would be better to make that the end of their
ride, and so turn round and go home. Phonny
and Malleville were quite desirous of going a
little farther, but Beechnut thought that he
should be tired by the time he reached the
house again.

"But you will not have time to finish the
story," said Phonny.

"Yes," replied Beechnut, "there is very little more to tell. It is only to give an account of our shipwreck."

"Why! did you have a shipwreck?" exclaimed Phonny.

"Yes," said Beechnut. "When you have turned the wagon, I will tell you about it."

So Phonny, taking a great sweep, turned the wagon round, and the party set their faces toward home. The Marshall was immediately going to set out upon a trot, but Phonny held him back by pulling upon the reins, and saying,

"Steady, Marshall! steady! You have got to walk all the way home."

"The storm drove us upon the Nova Scotia coast," said Beechnut, resuming his story. "We did not know any thing about the great danger that we were in, until just before the ship went ashore. When we got near the shore, the sailors put down all the anchors, but they would not hold, and, at length, the ship struck. Then there followed a dreadful scene of consternation and confusion. Some jumped into the sea in their terror, and were drowned. Some cried and screamed, and acted as if they were insane. Some were calm, and behaved

rationally.   The sailors opened the hatches and
let the passengers come up, and we got into the
most sheltered places that we could find about
the decks and rigging, and tied ourselves to
whatever was nearest at hand.   My father
opened his trunk and took out his two clock
weights, and gave me one of them.   The other
he kept himself.   He told me that we might as
well *try* to save them, though he did not suppose that we should be able to do so.

"Pretty soon after we struck, the storm
seemed to abate a little.   The people of the
country came down to the shore and stood upon
the rocks, to see if they could do any thing to
save us.   We were very near the shore, but the
breakers and the boiling surf were so violent
between us and the land, that whoever took to
the water was sure to be dashed in pieces.   So
every body clung to the ship, waiting for the
captain to contrive some way to get us to the
shore."

"And what did he do?" asked Phonny.

"He first got a long line and a cask, and he
fastened the end of the long line to the cask, and
then threw the cask overboard.   The other end
of the line was kept on board the ship.   The cask
was tossed about upon the waves, every suc-

cessive surge driving it in nearer and nearer to the shore, until at last it was thrown up high upon the rocks. The men upon the shore ran to seize it, but before they could get hold of it, the receding wave carried it back again among the breakers, where it was tossed about as if it had been a feather, and overwhelmed with the spray. Presently away it went again up upon the shore, and the men again attempted to seize it. This was repeated two or three times. At last they succeeded in grasping hold of it, and they ran up with it upon the rocks, out of the reach of the seas.

"The captain then made signs to the men to pull the line in toward the shore. He was obliged to use signs, because the roaring and thundering of the seas made such a noise, that nothing could be heard. The sailors had before this, under the captain's direction, fastened a much stronger line, a small cable in fact, to the end of the line which had been attached to the barrel. Thus, by pulling upon the smaller line, the men drew one end of the cable to the shore. The other end remained on board the ship, while the middle of it lay tossing among the breakers between the ship and the shore.

"The scamen then carried that part of the

cable which was on ship-board up to the mast-head, while the men on shore made their end fast to a very strong post which they set in the ground. The seamen drew the cable as tight as they could, and fastened their end very strongly to the mast-head. Thus the line of the cable passed in a gentle slope from the top of the mast to the land high above all the surges and spray.

" The captain then rigged what he called a sling, which was a sort of loop of ropes that a person could be put into and made to slide down in it on the cable, to the shore. A great many of the passengers were afraid to go in this way, but they were still more afraid to remain on board the ship."

" What were they afraid of?" asked Phonny.

" They were afraid," replied Beechnut, " that the shocks of the seas would soon break the ship to pieces, and then they would all be thrown into the sea together. In this case they would certainly be destroyed ; for if they were no. drowned, they would be dashed to pieces on the rocks which lined the shore."

Sliding down the line seemed thus a very dangerous attempt, but they consented one

after another, to make the trial, and thus we all
escaped safe to land."

THE WRECK.

"And did you get the clock-weights safe to
the shore?" asked Phonny.

"Yes," replied Beechnut, "and as soon as
we landed we hid them in the sand. My father
took me to a little cove close by, where there
was not much surf, as the place was protected
by a rocky point of land which bounded it upon
one side. Behind this point of land the waves
rolled up quietly upon a sandy beach. My

I

father went down upon the slope of this beach
to a place a little below where the highest waves
came, and began to dig a hole in the sand. He
called me to come and help him. The waves
impeded our work a little, but we persevered
until we had dug a hole about a foot deep. We
put our clock-weights into this hole and covered
them over. We then ran back up upon the
beach. The waves that came up every mo·
ment over the place, soon smoothed the surface
of the sand again, and made it look as if nothing had been done there. My father measured
the distance from the place where he had deposi-
ted his treasure, up to a certain great white
rock upon the shore exactly opposite to it, so as
to be able to find the place again, and then we
went back to our company. They were collected on the rocks in little groups, wet and
tired, and in great confusion—but rejoiced at
having escaped with their lives. Some of the
last of the sailors were then coming over in the
sling. The captain himself came last of all.

" There were some huts near the place, on the
shore, where the men built good fires, and we
warmed and dried ourselves. The storm aba-
ted a great deal in a few hours, and the tide
went down, so that we could go off to the ship

before night to get some provisions. The next morning the men could work at the ship very easily, and they brought all the passenger's baggage on shore. My father got his trunk with the clock in it. A day or two afterward some sloops came to the place, and took us all away to carry us to Quebec. Just before we embarked on board the sloops, my father and I, watching a good opportunity, dug up our weights out of the sand, and put them back safely in their places in the clock-box."

"Is that the end?" asked Phonny, when Beechnut paused.

"Yes," replied Beechnut, "I believe I had better make that the end.".

"I think it is a very interesting story," said Malleville. " And do you feel very tired?"

"No," said Beechnut. "On the contrary, I feel all the better for my ride. I believe I will sit up a little while." So saying, he raised himself in the wagon, and sat up, and began to look about him.

" What a wonderful voyage you had, Beechnut," said Phonny. " But I never knew before that you were ship-wrecked."

" Well, in point of fact," replied Beechnut, "I never was ship-wrecked "

"Never was!" exclaimed Phonny. "Why, what is all this story that you have been telling us then?"

"Embellishment," said Beechnut, quietly.

"Embellishment!" repeated Phonny, more and more amazed.

"Yes," said Beechnut.

"Then you were not wrecked at all?" said Phonny.

"No," replied Beechnut.

"And how did you get to the land?" asked Phonny.

"Why, we sailed quietly up the St. Lawrence," replied Beechnut, "and landed safely at Quebec, as other vessels do."

"And the clock-weights?" asked Phonny.

"All embellishment," said Beechnut. "My father had no such clock, in point of fact. He put his money in a bag, his bag in his chest, and his chest in the hold, and it came as safe as the captain's sextant."

"And the iceberg and the rainbow?" said Malleville.

"Embellishment, all embellishment," said Beechnut.

"Dear me!" said Phonny, "I thought it was all true."

"Did you?" said Beechnut. "I am sorry that you were so deceived; and I am sure it was not my fault, for I gave you your choice of a true story or an invention, and you chose the invention."

"Yes," said Phonny, "so we did."

Soon after this the whole party arrived safely at home.

134 BEECHNUT.

Discussion between Phonny and Malleville. Malleville's health.

CHAPTER VII.

SICKNESS.

THERE was some debate between Phonny and Malleville after they got home from their ride with Beechnut, on the question whether it was best to have stories embellished or not. Phonny could not help feeling a little vexed with himself at having been so completely deceived in listening to Beechnut's narrative of his voyage, especially after having been so distinctly warned by Beechnut as to what the character of the narrative was to be. Malleville said that she liked embellished stories, because they were so interesting. Phonny, on the whole, assented to this opinion, though he said that it was a great pity that stories could not be interesting and true too.

Malleville, who was always a very feeble child in respect to health, was attacked with a very serious fit of sickness at one time, a month or two after Beechnut recovered from his hurt, and what made her case the more serious, the sickness occurred at a time when her aunt Henry was away from home. Mr. Henry, her uncle, was almost always away, being required to be so by his business. Sometimes he would come home, and after remaining a few days at Franconia he would go away again, taking Mrs. Henry with him, and be gone two or three weeks. It was during one of these absences of Mrs. Henry from home that Malleville was attacked with the sickness.

The disease was the croup, a disease which is very distressing, and sometimes very dangerous. Malleville's attack came on in the night Beechnut mounted one of the horses, and galloped away a mile to the village to bring the doctor. Malleville was much worse before the doctor came. The doctor remained with her, prescribing for her, and taking care of her, for four or five hours. He came in a gig, and he brought his medicines with him in a small leathern case which he always carried with him in making his visits. Malleville was very patient and submissive, and made no difficulty about taking whatever the doctor prescribed. Thus, she was much sooner relieved of her distress than she would have been if she had been intractable and impatient, and had refused to take what Dr. Keep considered it necessary to give her.

Mr. and Mrs. Henry, when they went away, left Malleville and Phonny under the charge of the domestics, particularly of a girl named Hepzibah. Hepzibah was a very strong and capable girl, and very faithful and trustworthy. She was, moreover, very fond of Malleville, and was always very kind to her, whether she was sick or well. She, however, had never been sick herself, and she knew nothing about sickness. She slept in the next room to Malleville, and had been very much alarmed when Malleville was taken sick. She was in great trepidation until the doctor came, and she was very eager and earnest in aiding him in all that he did, and in bringing immediately all that he called for. She felt, at last, very happy when she found that Malleville was relieved, and was likely soon to be decidedly better. In fact, about three o'clock in the morning Malleville breathed almost as well as ever, and soon after that she fell into a quiet sleep. The doctor then said he thought that the difficulty was over, and that he would go away. He would come again, however, he said, immediately after breakfast, to see if any thing more was required.

He told Hepzibah, as he went away, that it was always very painful to him to see young children in distress, but that the pain was very much diminished when the child that was suffering was so patient, and submissive, and tractable as Malleville had been. Malleville was asleep when the doctor said this, but Hepzibah determined that she would tell her of it as soon as she awoke. She, accordingly, did so, and Malleville was very much gratified at hearing it.

After breakfast, Dr. Keep called again, according to his promise. He found Malleville a great deal better. The doctor left some drops in a phial, which he directed that she should take from time to time during the day, and also some powders which she must take toward evening, if she should then appear restless and feverish. He said, too, that she must be kept pretty quiet during the day.

Malleville slept most of the forenoon, and at dinner time she seemed better even than she had been in the morning. She asked to be allowed to get up and be dressed, and to play with Phonny. Hepzibah, accordingly, dressed her.

and Phonny brought his playthings into the room to play with her. He also, by permission from Hepzibah, went and invited one of Malleville's playmates, named Sarah, who lived at not a great distance from Mrs. Henry's, to come and help him amuse her. Sarah came, and for two or three hours the children enjoyed themselves very much. Malleville was, however, too weak to bear the excitement and exertion which the play they were engaged in often led to; and several times, as she sat with Phonny and Sarah upon the carpet, she would lay her head down upon a sofa-cushion which was near her, and seem very tired.

At last, she got up from the carpet, and went to the bed and lay down upon it. Phonny and Sarah went on with their playing, speaking now and then to Malleville to call her attention to something that they were doing. In such cases she would raise her head a moment to look, and then immediately afterward lay it down again, as if she were very tired.

About four o'clock, Beechnut concluded to go up to her room and see how she was. He had been at work in the garden, and as he left the garden to go up into Malleville's room, he gathered a small bouquet of beautiful flowers to give to her. He went up the stairs to her room and knocked at the door.

"Come in," said Phonny, in a loud voice.

"Ah, Beechnut!" said Phonny, as soon as the door opened, "is it you? I am glad you have come, for I want you to see my rail-road train."

Phonny had a row of books upon the carpet, which he called his rail-road train.

"This is the baggage-car," continued Phonny, "and this the locomotive; choo—choo—choo—choo."

Beechnut paid no attention to Phonny, but walked directly across the room to Malleville's bedside.

Malleville's face looked flushed and feverish, and she was tossing restlessly to and fro. She did not speak to Beechnut. Beechnut did not speak to her. He did not even offer her the bouquet of flowers, but held it behind him where she should not see it. In such a state as she evidently was in, the trouble of taking a bouquet of flowers, and saying, "I thank you," for them, is sometimes a great burden. Beechnut knew all about this, for he had often been sick himself.

He looked at Malleville a moment, and put his hand gently upon her head, and then looked round and took a survey of the room. The floor was covered with the litter of books and playthings that Phonny had scattered around, and with chips and shavings, near the fire-place, which he had made there in an attempt to fabricate some *juck-straws* for Malleville. There was a table by the side of the bed covered with phials, and jars, and cups, which had had medicine in them, and with bowls partly filled with arrow-root and gruel. The bed was very much tumbled, the linen being more or less soiled and stained with the spillings of the medicine that had been administered in haste the night before. The room felt a little chilly too, as it had been a cool autumnal day, and the sun which had made it warm and cheerful during the morning, now no longer shone in at the windows.

Beechnut surveyed this comfortless scene of confusion for a few minutes, as if hesitating what plan he should adopt for effecting a revolution.

At length, after a moment's pause, he went to Phonny, and speaking to him in a low voice, he asked him to come out into the entry.

"Phonny," said he, "could you do me a favor?"

"Why,—ves,—" said Phonny, doubtfully;

"only Sarah wants me to stay and play cars with her."

"What I want you to do," said Beechnut, "is to go away for me on some business in the wagon."

"Oh, yes," said Phonny; "certainly. I will go. Wait a minute till I go and tell Sarah."

"Stop a moment," said Beechnut, "until you get your directions. Go and tell Sarah in a whisper, that you are going away for me in a wagon, and that if she would like to go with you she can. Then leave all your books and play-things just as they are, on the floor, and go down into the yard and wait there until I come."

"Well," said Phonny, "I will." Phonny was always greatly pleased with the idea of going away on business in the wagon: no mat ter where he went, or what the business might be

So Beechnut and Phonny returned into Malleville's room. Phonny went to whisper his message to Sarah, and Beechnut returned to Malleville's bedside again.

"Malleville," said Beechnut, "should you like to have Mary Bell come and see you a little while?"

"Yes," said Malleville, "very much indeed."

"Only I am afraid," said Beechnut, "that it

will make too much company for you. Do you think you would be willing to stay alone a little while till I can send for Mary Bell, for the sake of having her come and see you?"

"Yes," said Malleville, "very willing indeed."

"Then I will send for her," said Beechnut. "But she will not be able to stay with you very long, for her mother is sick, and she cannot be away from home a great while."

"No matter," said Malleville, "I should like to have her come."

So Beechnut drew up a little table to the side of the bed, and put a bell upon it for Malleville to ring in case she should want any thing while she was alone. If she rang the bell, Hepzibah, Beechnut said, would hear it, and would come. Then Beechnut went away.

He found Phonny and Sarah waiting for him in the yard. He immediately harnessed the horse into the wagon, and then helped Phonny and Sarah to get into it. He directed Phonny to drive to Mrs. Bell's, to tell Mary that Malleville was sick, and to ask her if she could not get into the wagon, and come and see her for half an hour. He would take her back again in the wagon, Phonny was to say, as soon as she was ready to go.

"Sarah can go with you to Mary Bell's," said
Beechnut, in closing his instructions, "and then
you can leave her at her own home on the way
back."

Phonny, after receiving these directions,
drove away. In about three quarters of an
hour he returned, bringing Mary Bell with him.

Beechnut went to meet the wagon as it drove
up to the door, and helped Mary Bell to get out.
He told her that he was sorry to send for her,
as he knew that her mother was sick, but that
Malleville was restless and not very comfortable in her room, and he thought that she would
probably have a better night, if somebody who
was more accustomed to sickness than Hepzibah, could see her a little while, and make ar
rangements.

"Yes," said Mary Bell, "I am very glad that
you sent for me."

Mary Bell took off her bonnet and put it upon
the parlor-table, and then went directly up into
Malleville's room. She had often visited Malleville, and had often taken care of her when
she was sick, so she knew exactly where to go.

Malleville's eyes were shut, and she was almost asleep when Mary Bell came in, but she
was in an uneasy and uncomfortable position,

and she looked flushed and feverish. Mary
went softly up to her bedside, but did not speak
a word. Presently she reclined herself upon
the bed, and after placing her cheek close to
Malleville's for a moment, she kissed her very
gently, laying her hand at the same time upon
Malleville's shoulder. Malleville opened her
eyes, and when she saw that it was Mary Bell,
she put her arm around Mary Bell's neck, but
did not speak. Mary Bell remained in that position a minute or two longer, then gently dis-
engaged herself, saying, in a whisper, " Lie still ·
I am coming back again, presently."

Mary Bell then went down stairs to find Hepzibah. She told her that she had come to see
Malleville, and that she was very sorry that she
could not stay all night and help take care of
her.

"You must be very tired," said she to Hepzibah, "after being up with Malleville all last
night, and having all your work to do to-day.
However, I will stay a little while, and get her
ready for the night."

" I shall be very glad if you will," said Hepzibah, " for I don't know much about sickness.
Whatever you want, tell me, and I will get it
for you."

"All I shall want," said Mary Bell, "is some warm water in the little bathing-tub. Every thing else I can get myself. And when you bring the water up, you may bring down the things that I put out into the entry. I will put out all the things that will not be wanted in the night."

So Mary Bell went back to Malleville's room. The first thing that she did was to gather up all the books and play-things that Phonny had left scattered about the room, and put them away. The books she put in their places upon the shelves, and the play-things she put in the basket where they belonged, and carried them into Phonny's play-room. Then she took all the medicines, and phials, and bowls, and spoons, and put them upon the great waiter, and set them out into the entry for Hepzibah to carry away. A few things, those which she thought it possible might be used in the night, she reserved ; but she put every thing which she thus reserved, upon a small light-stand, in neat order, after first spreading a clean towel over the light-stand, and then placed the stand at the foot of the bed, where the foot-board would conceal it from Malleville's view. She then put all the furniture of the room in its proper order, and swept up

K

the chips and shavings that Phonny had left in
the corner.   The room now looked very cheerful and had lost entirely the appearance of a
sick-chamber.   There was a very pleasant little
fire burning in the fire-place. Beechnut had
made it while Phonny was bringing Mary Bell.

By the time that Mary Bell had finished putting the room in order, Hepzibah came up with
the little bathing-tub, which was a small tub
that Mrs. Henry was accustomed to use for a
foot-bath.   Mary Bell took the tub, and put it
upon a chair by the side of the bed.   She told
Hepzibah that she might take down the things
which were upon the waiter, in the entry, and
she requested her also when she went down, to
ask Beechnut to bring up a little more wood for
the fire.

She then went to the bedside, and took off
Malleville's shoes and stockings, and then gently
moved her to the edge of the bed, and placed
her in such a position that her feet hung down
by the side of the bed, so that she could put
them into the bathing-tub.   The water was
very warm, but not too hot, and Malleville evidently liked the feeling of it very much, the moment that her feet were put in.   Mary Bell left
Malleville's feet in the water, and went to the

bureau, where the linen was kept, and took out some fresh sheets and pillow-cases, and also a night-dress for Malleville. These she hung over a chair by the fire, to air and warm them. Then she came back to Malleville, and began to bathe her feet in the warm water, by means of a great sponge. She poured more hot water into the little tub, from time to time, so as to preserve the temperature of the bath at the right point. When she had bathed the feet sufficiently, she wiped them very dry with a hot towel, one that she had taken from the bureau, and put to the fire with the other linen. Malleville lay perfectly still during the whole operation, and did not speak a word.

Mary Bell then undressed Malleville, and put her night-dress upon her. She then moved a sofa which was standing at the back side of the room, up before the fire, and put the cushions at one end of it, and a pillow on the cushions. Then she came back to the bedside and said,

"Now, Malleville, I am going to carry you to the fire."

"Oh, no," said Malleville. "You must not carry me. I can walk. I feel a great deal better."

But Mary Bell insisted upon carrying her

patient, for fear, as she said, that she might
take cold in stepping upon the floor ; though, as
there was a good warm carpet upon the floor,
perhaps there was not much danger of this. So
Malleville kneeled up upon the side of the bed,
and Mary Bell took her and carried her to the
fire. She laid her down upon the sofa, with her
head upon the pillow.

" There," said Mary Bell, " lie there still, while
I make your bed."

Mary Bell then proceeded to make the bed,
while Malleville lay upon the sofa, watching
the fire.

When Mary Bell had made the bed, and had
put the linen which she had taken off from it
out into the entry for Hepzibah to carry away,
she came back to the sofa where Malleville was
lying, bringing with her a soft towel and a cup
half full of cool water, with a little cologne in
it. She placed the cup upon the little light-
stand at the foot of the bed, which, as it happened, was very near the sofa. She then proceeded to bathe Malleville's face and hands
with the water, and to wipe them gently with
the soft towel. She then combed her hair for
a long time with a large toothed comb, sometimes combing it forward and sometimes back,

but moving the comb very gently every time. Malleville lay perfectly still while she was doing this. In fact, Mary Bell thought at one time that she was asleep. She was, however, undeceived by Malleville's opening her eyes and asking in a somewhat mournful tone,

"Mary Bell, do you think that I am going to be very sick?"

"No," replied Mary Bell. "I think you are going to get well."

"Do you!" said Malleville. "I am glad of that."

At last, Mary Bell took Malleville up again from the sofa and carried her to her bed. The fresh, clean sheets, warm from the fire, felt very grateful to Malleville's feverish frame as Mary Bell covered her up in them, and they produced a very soothing and calming effect.

Mary Bell then went and brought Malleville's little Bible, and sat down by the head of the bed.

"Now," said she, "I am going to read you some verses from the Bible and hear you say your prayer, and then I want you to go to sleep."

"Well," said Malleville, "I will, if I can."

Mary Bell then opened the Bible, and read a

few verses from the Psalms. Then she shut
the book, and putting her arm around Malleville's neck, she laid her own head down upon
the pillow by Malleville's side, and Malleville
repeated her prayer. After thus repeating the
form which she was accustomed to use, she
added some special petitions of her own. She
prayed that God would make her patient in her
sickness, and cause her to get well: and that
he would take care of her uncle and aunt, who
were away, and bring them home again in
safety. She also prayed for her father and
mother, and all her other friends, that God
would watch over them all, and prepare them
all for happiness in heaven.

When the prayer was ended, Mary Bell
kissed Malleville again, and said that now she
must go away.

"I must go back," said she, "and take care
of my mother. I shall tell her how patient and
gentle you are, and she will feel glad. You
must lie still and go to sleep, if you can. I
will send Phonny to come and sit here with
you, if you wish to have him come, but you
must not talk to him. He must sit by the fire
and read, and be still, so that you may go to
sleep."

" Well," said Malleville.

"By-and-by," continued Mary Bell, "after you have been asleep an hour, you may wake up again, if you wish to, and if you feel pretty well then, perhaps Beechnut will come in and tell you a story. It will be better for you to be awake awhile by-and-by—you will sleep so much better in the night for it."

So Mary Bell went to call Phonny, that he might come and sit in Malleville's room. It was now nearly dark, and Mary Bell, therefore, closed the shutters, and brought in a small lamp for Phonny to read by. She put this lamp upon the little light-stand at the foot of the bed, where it would be shaded by the foot-board and curtains from Malleville's eyes. She moved the sofa back into its place, and placed a small rocking-chair near the stand for Phonny to sit in. It was a very pleasant place indeed to sit and read.

When all was thus arranged, Mary Bell went once more to Malleville's bedside, and kissed her, and bade her good night. Malleville shut up her eyes, and soon went to sleep. She slept so soundly, that when about an hour afterward the doctor came to see her, he went to her bed-side, and after looking at her a few moments and gently feeling of her pulse, he said that she was doing very well, and that he would not disturb her.

MALLEVILLE ASLEEP.

When Malleville went to sleep, it was with the full determination of waking up again in half an hour, and sending for Beechnut to come and tell her a story. She did not, however, wake up for more than two hours. When she did wake, she found herself alone. Phonny had got tired of reading some time before, and perceiving that Malleville was asleep, he had got up from his rocking-chair and walked away softly out of the room.

CHAPTER VIII.

AGNES.

MALLEVILLE was very much refreshed by
her sleep. When she awoke, she was at first a
little startled to find herself alone, and she was
inclined at once to reach out her hand to the
bell and ring it for the purpose of calling Hepzibah; but on considering what she should say
that she wanted when Hepzibah should come,
she found herself a little puzzled, inasmuch as
she did not want any thing. So she lay still a
moment musing.

The room looked so pleasantly in consequence of the arrangements that Mary Bell had
made, that Malleville soon ceased to feel uneasy
at being left alone in it. Every thing was in
order, and the lamp which Phonny had left
burning upon the stand diffused a gentle but
cheerful illumination around the apartment.
The light of the fire, too, which glowed warmly
upon that part of the ceiling which Malleville
saw between the curtains of her bed, in a

genial, though variable and flickering light, seemed to dispel all sense of loneliness from her mind.

"I will wait a few minutes," said Malle-ville to herself. "Perhaps Phonny will come back again."

So she left the bell where it was upon the table, and began to sing a little song. It was a song that Beechnut had taught her.

After singing a little while she raised herself in the bed and sat up, leaning against the pillows and bolsters which she piled up behind her to furnish a support. She sat in this position a few minutes, looking about the room between the curtains of the bed which she had pushed aside.

"How pleasant it is!" said she to herself. "That is because Mary Bell has been here. And how much better I feel!"

The thought then occurred to her, that she would creep along to the foot of the bed and look between the curtains over the foot-board. It was possible, she thought, that Phonny might be there asleep. She, accordingly, did so, but she found that Phonny was not there. The rocking-chair was standing in its place by the side of the light-stand, empty. The lamp was

AGNES. 155

Malleville goes to look at Phonny's book.   Beechnut.

upon the stand, and the book which Phonny
had been reading was lying spread open upside
down upon the stand near the lamp. When
Phonny went away, he had intended to return
in a few minutes and finish his reading; and so
he had left his book.

Malleville's curiosity was excited to know
what book it was that Phonny had been read·
ing, and whether there were any pretty pictures
in it. So she slid down off the bed, and went
to the rocking-chair. She took the precaution
to put on her stockings by the way, and then
resting her feet upon a little cricket that was
there, in such a position that they were turned
toward the fire, she took the book and began
to look at the pictures.

In a few minutes she heard some one gently
tapping at the door. She said, "Come in."
The door opened, and the visitor proved to be
Beechnut. He looked surprised to see Malleville up, but said that he was glad to see it, if
it was an indication that she was better.

"I am better," replied Malleville, "a great
dea. better, and I am very glad that you have
come, for Mary Bell said that you might come
this evening and tell me a story. I wish you
would sit down and tell it to me now."

158   BEECHNUT.

Beechnut must change his dress.   He goes away.

"Not just now," said Beechnut. "You must have some supper first. And then, if I am coming in here to tell you a story, I must go and get ready."

"Get ready?" repeated Malleville. "Why, you are all ready now."

"No," said Beechnut, "I must go and change my dress."

Beechnut was always very careful about his dress and appearance, even when at his work; and he looked particularly neat and tidy now, so that Malleville saw no necessity for any change. Beechnut, however, said that though his dress, as it was, would do well enough for his work, yet that he could not think of coming to visit a young lady without making suitable preparations. Finally, he recommended to Malleville to go back to her bed again, and promised to send Hepzibah up to bring her some supper. "Then," said he, "in about half an hour, when you have had your supper, and are all ready for the night, I will come and talk you to sleep by telling you a story."

Beechnut then went away, and Malleville went back to her bed. In a short time Hepzibah came up with some tea and toast, upon a waiter, for Malleville's supper. Besides the tea and toast, there was a small glass dish upon the waiter, covered up, so that Malleville could not see what was under it. She took the cover off of this dish the first thing when the waiter was brought to her, to see what was there; she found that it was currant jelly.

Phonny came into the room just after Hepzibah, and stood by Malleville's bedside while she ate her supper. He had had his own supper before, but Malleville gave him some of her toast and currant jelly.

"Is the doctor coming to see me again tonight, Hepzibah?" asked Malleville.

"No," said Hepzibah, "not again. He came while you were asleep. He says that you are doing very well, and there is nothing more for you to take, except that there are some drops in a phial that I am to give you about half-past ten, if you don't breathe easily."

Here Malleville drew a very long breath, to see if she could breathe easily then. She said she could breathe very easily indeed, and she did not think that she should have to take the drops. Then Phonny began to take long breaths, as if to see whether his lungs were in good condition. This induced Malleville to repeat her experiment, and for several minutes the children kept up such a panting and sighing, that Hepzibah told them that they were wasting all their breath, and that if Malleville was not careful, she would not have enough left to last till morning.

When Malleville had finished her supper, Hepzibah carried the waiter down stairs again, and in about half an hour Beechnut came in.

" Now Phonny," said Malleville, " here comes Beechnut, to tell me a story, and you must not interrupt us.   This story is to be for me alto-gether."

"Can't you let me stay and hear it?" asked Phonny. ·

" Yes," replied Malleville, " you may stay, if you will not interrupt us.   And Beechnut," con-.inued Malleville, " I wish that you would take me into your arms and rock me while you are telling the story.   I am tired of lying in this bed so long."

" Well," said Beechnut.   " I will go and get a rocking-chair."

The rocking-chair which Phonny had been sitting in was too small for Beechnut's purpose.

In a few minutes Beechnut returned with a large rocking-chair, which he placed by the fire, on one side.   He then took Malleville in his arms and carried her to the chair, and sat down. Next he asked Phonny to go out into the entry, and look by the side of the door, and to bring in what he should find there.

"What is it?" asked Malleville.

"You will see." replied Beechnut. So saying, he placed Malleville in his lap in such a position that she could see the door and the fire. Her head rested upon a small pillow which Beechnut had laid upon his shoulder. By the time that Malleville was thus placed, Phonny came back. He had in his hand a small sheet-iron pan, with three large and rosy apples in it. Beechnut directed Phonny to put this pan down upon the hearth where the apples would roast.

"Who are they for?" asked Malleville.

"One is for you," replied Beechnut, "one for Phonny, and one for me. But we are not going to eat them till to-morrow morning."

"There ought to be one for Hepzibah,' said Malleville.

"Why, Hepzibah can get as many apples as she wants," said Beechnut, "and roast them whenever she pleases.—Only," he continued, after a moment's pause, "perhaps it would please her to have us remember her, and roast her one together with ours."

"Yes," said Phonny. "I think it would."

"Then," said Beechnut, "you may go, Phonny, and get her an apple. You can make room for one more upon the pan."

"Well," said Phonny; "but you must not begin the story until I come back."

So Phonny went away to get an apple for Hepzibah. In a short time he returned, bringing with him a very large and beautiful apple, which he put upon the pan with the rest. There was just room for it. He then set the pan down before the fire, and took his own seat in the little rocking-chair, which still stood in its place by the side of the light-stand.

"Now, Beechnut," said he, as soon as he was seated, "now for the story."

"What sort of a story shall I tell you, Malleville?" asked Beechnut. "Shall it be the plain truth, or shall it be embellished?"

"Embellished," said Malleville. "I wish you would embellish it as much as ever you can."

"Well," said Beechnut, "I will tell you about Agnes."

"Agnes!" repeated Phonny, "who was she?"

"You must not speak, Phonny" said Malleville. "Beechnut is going to tell this story to me."

"Yes," said Beechnut, "it is altogether for Malleville, and you must not say a word about it from beginning to end."

"One night," continued Beechnut, "abou three weeks ago, I sat up very late in my room, writing. It was just after I got well from my hurt, and as I had been kept away from my desk for a long time, I was very glad to get back to it again, and I used to sit up quite late in the evenings, writing and reading. The night that I am now speaking of, I sat up even later than usual. It had been a very warm day, and the evening air, as it came into my open window, was cool and delightful. Besides, there was a bright moon, and it shone very brilliantly upon the garden, and upon the fields and mountains beyond, as I looked upon them from my window.

"At last, I finished my writing just as the clock struck twelve, and as I still did not feel sleepy, notwithstanding that it was so late, and as the night was so magnificent, I thought that I would go out and take a little walk. So I put my books and papers away, took my cap and put it upon my head, and then stepped out

of the window upon the roof of the shed, which,
you know, is just below it.   I thought it better
to go out that way rather than to go down
the stairs, as by going down the stairs I
might possibly have disturbed somebody in the
house.

"I walked along the roof of the shed, without meeting any body or seeing any body except Moma.   She was lying down asleep behind one of the chimneys."

Moma was a large black cat belonging to
Malleville.

"Poor Moma!" said Malleville.   "Has not
she got any better place to sleep in than that?
I mean to make her a bed, as soon as I get
well."

"When I reached the end of the shed," continued Beechnut, "I climbed down by the grea
trellis, to the fence, and from the fence to the
ground.   I went along the yard to the steps of
the south platform, and sat down there.   I
looked very pleasant in the garden, and I went
in there.   I walked through the garden and out
at the back gate, into the woods, and so up the
glen.   I rambled along different glens and val-
leys for half an hour, until at last I came to a
most beautiful place among groves and thickets

where there was a large spring boiling out from under some mossy rocks.   The spring was in a deep shady place, and was overhung with beautiful trees.   In front of the spring was a large basin of water, half as large as this room.   The water was very clear, and as the moonlight shone upon it through the interstices of the trees, I could see that the bottom was covered with yellow sands, while beautiful shells and pebbles lined the shore.

" The water fell down into the basin from the spring in a beautiful cascade.   All around there were a great many tall wild flowers growing. It seemed to me the most beautiful place that I ever saw.   I sat down upon a large round stone which projected out from a grassy bank just below this little dell, where I could see the basin of water, and the spring, and the flowers upon its banks, and could hear the sound of the water falling over the cascade.

" There was a very large oak-tree growing near the basin, upon one side.   I could only see the lower part of the stem of it.   The top was high in the air, and was concealed from view by the foliage of the thickets.   The stem of the tree was very large indeed, and it had a very ancient and venerable appearance.   There was a hollow place in this tree very near the ground, which had in some degree the appearance of a door, arched above. The sides of this opening were fringed with beautiful green moss, which hung down within it like a curtain, and there were a great many beautiful flowers growing upon each side of it. Another thing which attracted my attention and excited my curiosity very strongly was, that there seemed to be a little path leading from this door down to the margin of the water.

" While I was wondering what this could mean, I suddenly observed that there was a waving motion in the long moss which hung down within the opening in the trunk of the tree, and presently I saw a beautiful little face peeping out. I was of course very much astonished, but I determined to sit perfectly still, and see what would happen.

" I was in such a place that the person to whom the face belonged could not see me, though I could see her perfectly. After look-ing about for a minute or two timidly, she came out. She was very beautiful indeed, with her dark hair hanging in curls upon her neck and shoulders. Her dress was very simple, and yet it was very rich and beautiful.

" What did she have on ?" asked Malleville.

" Why, I don't know that I can describe it very well," said Beechnut. " I am not much accustomed to describe ladies' dresses. It was, however, the dress of a child. She had in her hand a very long feather, like a peacock's feather, only, instead of being of many colors, it was white, like silver ; and it had the luster of silver. I verily believe it must have been made of silver."

" I don't believe it would be possible," said Phonny, " to make a feather of silver."

" Why not ?" asked Beechnut, " as well as make a tassel of glass. However, it *looked* like silver, and it was extremely graceful and brilliant as she held it in her hands waving in the moonbeams.

" After looking about for a minute or two, and seeing nobody, she began to dance down the little path to the brink of the basin, and when she reached it she began to speak. Now,' said she, 'I'll freeze the fountain, and then i'll have a dance.'

" As she said this, she stood upon the pebbles of the shore, and began gently to draw the tip of her long feather over the surface of the water ; and I saw to my amazement, that wher-

ever the feather passed it changed the surface
of the water into ice. Long feathery crystals
began to shoot in every direction over the basin,
wherever Agnes moved her wand."

" Was her name Agnes ?" asked Malleville.

" Yes," said Beechnut.

" How did you know ?" asked Malleville.

" Oh, she told me afterward," replied Beechnut. " You will hear how presently. When
she had got the surface of the water frozen, she
stepped cautiously upon it to see if it would
bear."

" Would it ?" asked Malleville.

" Yes," replied Beechnut, " it bore her perfectly. She advanced to the middle of it,
springing up and down upon her feet to try the
strength of the ice as she proceeded. She found
that it was very strong.

" ' Now,' said she, ' for the cascade.'

" So saying, she began to draw her silver
feather down the cascade, and immediately the
same effect was produced which I had observed
before upon the water. The noise of the
water-fall was immediately hushed. Beautiful
stalactites and icicles were formed in the place
of the pouring and foaming water. I should
have thought that the cascade had been wholly

congealed were it not that I could see in some places by the moonlight that the water was still gurgling down behind the ice, just as it usually does when cascades and water-falls are frozen by natural cold."

"Yes," said Phonny. "I have watched it very often on the brook."

"On what brook?" asked Malleville.

"On the pasture brook," said Phonny.

Beechnut took no notice of Phonny's remark, but went on with his narrative as follows:

"Agnes then walked back and forth upon the ice, and began to draw the tip of her long silver feather over the branches of the trees that overhung the basin, and over the mossy banks, and the tall grass and flowers. Every thing that she touched turned into the most beautiful frost-work. The branches of the trees were loaded with snow. The banks hung with icicles, and the tall grass and flowers seemed to turn white and transparent, and they glittered in the moonbeams as if they were encrusted with diamonds. I never saw any thing so resplendent and beautiful.

"At last, she looked around upon it all, and said, 'There! that will do. I wonder now if the ice is strong enough.'

168 BEECHNUT.

She tries the ice.   Peep!   Beechnut's delight.

AGNES.

"Then she went into the middle of the ice.
and standing upon it on tiptoe, she sprang up
into the air, and then came down upon it again,
as if she were trying its strength. At the
same instant she said or sung in a beautiful sil-
very voice, like a bird, the word,

"'Peep!'

"When she had done this, she stopped a
moment to listen. I sat perfectly still, so as
not to let her know that I was near. Pres
ently, she leaped up again twice in succession,
singing,

" ' Peep!   Peep!'

" Then, after pausing a moment more, she began to dance away with the utmost agility and grace, singing all the time a little song, the music of which kept time with her dancing. This was the song :—

> " ' Peep! peep! chippeda dee,
> Playing in the moonlight—nobody to see ;
> The boys and girls are gone away,
> They've had their playtime in the day,
> And now the night is left to me.
> Peep! peep! chippeda dee.' "

" That's a pretty song," said Malleville.

" Yes," said Beechnut, " and you can not imagine how beautifully she sang it, and how gracefully she danced upon the ice while she was singing. I was so delighted that I could not sit perfectly still, but made some movement that caused a little rustling. Agnes stopped a moment to listen. I was very much afraid that she would see me. She did not see me, however, and so she began the second verse of her song.

> " ' Peep! peep! chippeda dee,
> The moon is for the mountains, the sun is for the sea ;'

" When she had got so far," continued Beechnut, "she suddenly stopped. She saw me. The fact was, I was trying to move back a little farther, so as to be more out of sight, and I made a little rustling, which she heard. The instant she saw me, she ran off the ice and up her little path to the opening in the oak, and in a moment disappeared. Presently, however, I saw the fringe of moss moving again, and she began to peep out.

" 'Beechnut,' said she, 'how came you here?'

" 'Why, I was taking a walk,' said I, 'and I came along this path. Don't you want me to be here?'

" 'No,' said she.

" 'Oh, then I will go away,' said I. 'But how came you to know me?'

" 'Oh, I know you very well,' said she. 'Your name is Beechnut.'

" 'And do you know Malleville?' said I.

" 'Yes,' said she. 'I know her very well. I like Malleville very much. I like her better than I do you'

" 'Ah!' said I. 'I am sorry for that. Why do you like her better than you do me?'

" 'Because she is a girl,' said Agnes.

" 'That is a good reason,' said I, 'I con

fess. I like girls myself better than I do boys. But how came you to know Malleville?'

" Oh, I have seen her a great many times,' said she, 'peeping into her windows by moonlight, when she was asleep.'

" 'Well," said I. 'I will tell Malleville about you, and she will want to come and see you.'

" 'No,' said Agnes, 'she must not come and see me ; but she may write me a letter.'

" 'But she is not old enough to write letters,' said I.

" 'Then,' said she, 'she must tell *you* what to write, and you must write it for her.' "

Beechnut observed, that though Phonny and Malleville neither of them spoke, they were both extremely interested, and somewhat excited by the story, and that he was far from accomplishing the object which he had in view at first in telling a story, namely, lulling Malleville to sleep. He, therefore, said to Malleville, that though he had a great deal more to tell her about Agnes, he thought it would be better not to tell any more then ; but that he would sing Agnes's song to her, to the same tune that Agnes herself sung it. He would sing it several times, he said, and she might listen, laying her head upon his shoulder.

Malleville said that she should like very much to hear Beechnut sing the song, but that after he had sung it, she hoped he would tell her a *little* more about Agnes that night. She liked to hear about her, she said, very much indeed.

So Beechnut changed Malleville's position placing her in such a manner that her head reclined upon his shoulder.

"Shut your eyes now," said he, "and form in your mind a picture of the little dell and fountain, with the frost-work beaming in the moonlight, and Agnes dancing on the ice, while I sing."

Then Beechnut began to sing the first verse of the song to a very lively and a very pretty tune. He could not sing the second verse, he said, because he had not heard it all. But the first verse he sung over and over again.

> "Peep! peep! chippeda dee!
> Playing in the moonlight, nobody to see
> The boys and girls have gone away,
> They've had their playtime in the day,
> And now the night is left for me,
> Peep! peep! chippeda dee!"

Malleville lay very still, listening to the song for about five minutes, and then Beechnut found that she was fast asleep. He then rose very gently, and carried her to her bed. He laid her in the bed, and Phonny, who stood by, covered her with the clothes. He and Phonny then crept softly out of the room

174   Beechnut.

Hepzibah goes to Malleville's room.   The clock.

Chapter IX.

A Sound Sleeper.

About nine o'clock, Hepzibah, having fin-ished her work for the day, covered up the kitchen fire, and fastened the outer doors. Beechnut had gone to bed, and so had Phonny. Hepzibah went into Phonny's room to see if all was safe, and to get the light. She then went into Malleville's room.

The room had a very pleasant aspect, al-though the fire had now nearly gone down. The lamp was burning on the stand at the foot of the bed where Phonny had left it. Hepzi-bah advanced softly to the bedside. Malleville was lying asleep there with her cheek upon her hand.

"Poor child!" said Hepzibah to herself "She has gone to sleep. What a pity that I have got to wake her up by-and-by, and give her some medicine."

Hepzibah then looked at a clock which stood upon the mantel-shelf, and saw that it was a little past nine. It was an hour or more before it would be time to give Malleville the drops. Hepzibah thought that if she went to bed, she should fall asleep, and not wake up again till morning, for she always slept very soundly. She determined, therefore, that she would sit up until half-past ten, and then, after giving Malleville the medicine, go to bed. She, accordingly, went and got her knitting-work, intending to keep herself awake while she sat up, by knitting. When she came back into the room, she began to look for a comfortable seat. She finally decided on taking the sofa.

Mary Bell, after using the sofa for Malleville while she was making the bed, had put it back into its place, by the side of the room. Hepzibah, however, easily brought it forward again, for it trundled very smoothly and noiselessly upon its castors. Hepzibah brought the sofa up to the fire, placing one end of it near to the stand, in order that she might have the benefit of the lamp in case of dropping a stitch. She prepared the medicine for Malleville, by mixing it properly with water in a little cup, and put it upon the stand, so that it should be all ready to be administered when the time should come, and then sat down upon the sofa, next to the sofa-cushions, which were upon the end of the sofa, between herself and the light.

Things went on very well for almost half an hour, but then Hepzibah being pretty tired in consequence of her long day's work, and of her want of rest the night before, began to grow sleepy. Twice her knitting-work dropped out of her hands. The dropping of the knitting-work waked her the first and second time that it occurred. But the third time it did not wake her. After falling half over and recovering herself two or three times, she at length sank down upon the cushions, with her head upon the uppermost of them, and there in a short time she was fast asleep.

She remained in this condition for nearly two hours, Malleville in her bed sleeping all the time quietly too. When Malleville went to sleep, she did so resolving not to wake up for her medicine. She did not resolve not to *take* it, if any one else waked her up for it, but she determined not to wake up for it of her own accord. Whether this had any influence in prolonging her sleep, it would be difficult to say. She did, however, sleep very soundly, and without changing her position at all, until a little after eleven o'clock, when she began to move her head and her arms a little, and presently she opened her eyes.

She looked around the room and saw nobody. The light was burning, though rather dimly, and the fire had nearly gone out. She sat up in the bed, and after a few minutes' pause she said in a gentle voice, as if speaking to herself,

"I wish there was somebody here to give me a drink of water." Then after waiting a moment, she added, "but I can just as well get down and find it myself."

So saying, she climbed down from the bed, and put on her shoes and stockings, singing gently all the time,

"Peep! peep! chippeda dee!"

This was all of Agnes' song that she could remember.

She went toward the fire, wondering who had drawn out the sofa and what for: and on passing round before it, her wonder was changed into amazement at finding Hepzibah asleep upon it.

"Why!" she exclaimed, in a very low and gentle tone, just above a whisper. "Here is Hepzibah. I suppose she is sitting up to watch with me. How tired she is!"

M

She stood looking at Hepzibah a minute or two in silence, and then said, speaking in the same tone and manner as before,

" She is not comfortable.   I mean to put her feet upon the sofa."

So saying, Malleville stooped down, and clasping Hepzibah's feet with both her arms she lifted them up as gently as she could, and put them upon the sofa.   Hepzibah's sound sleep was not at all disturbed by this.   In fact, her position being now much more easy than be fore, she sank away soon into a slumber deeper and more profound than ever.

Malleville finding that her first attempt to render Hepzibah a service was so successful, immediately began to feel a strong interest in taking care of her ; and observing that her feet were not very well covered, as she lay upon the sofa, she thought it would be a good plan to go and find something to cover them up.   So she went to a bureau which was standing in the room, and began to open one drawer after an- other in search of a small blanket which was sometimes used for such a purpose.   She found the blanket at length in the lowermost drawer of the bureau.

Malleville attempts to make a fire.

"Ah! here it is," said she. "I knew it was somewhere in this bureau."

Saying this, she took out the blanket and carried it to the sofa, doing every thing in as noiseless a manner as possible. She spread the blanket over Hepzibah's feet, tucking the edges under very gently and carefully all around.

"Now," said Malleville to herself, "I will make up the fire a little, so that she shall not catch cold."

There were two sticks remaining of those which Beechnut had brought up, and they were lying upon the carpet by the side of the fire, near the rocking-chair in which Beechnut had rocked Malleville to sleep. The wood which had been put upon the fire had burned entirely down, nothing being left of them but a few brands in the corners. Malleville took up the two sticks, one after another, and laid them upon the andirons, one for a back-stick and the other for a fore-stick, as she had often seen Phonny do. She then brought up a little cricket in front of the andirons, and sitting down upon it there, she took the tongs and began to pick up the brands and coals, and to put them into the interstice which was left between the two sticks. She did all this in a very noiseless and gentle manner, so as not to disturb Hepzibah; and she stopped very frequently to look round and see if Hepzibah was still sleeping.

The air soon began to draw up through the coals which Malleville had placed between the sticks of wood, and thus fanning them, it brightened them into a glow. The brands began to smoke, and presently there appeared in one part a small flickering flame.

"There!" said Malleville, in a tone of great satisfaction. "It is burning. Phonny said that I could not make a fire, but I knew that I could."

Malleville had been very careful all the time not to allow her night-dress to get near the fire, and now as the fire was beginning to burn, she thought that she must move still further away. She accordingly rose and moved the cricket back. The fire burned more and more brightly, and Malleville observed that the light of it was flashing upon Hepzibah's face.

"I must make a screen for her," said she "or the flashes will wake her up."

So she went to the bureau again and brought forth a shawl, one which she had often seen her aunt Henry use for this purpose. Then putting a chair between the sofa and the fire, she spread the shawl upon the back of it, and found that it produced the effect of keeping the flashes of light from Hepzibah's face, entirely to her sat. isfaction.

Malleville then began to wonder whether it was not time for her to take her medicine. She looked at the clock to see if she could tell what o'clock it was. She could not, of course, for she had never learned to tell the time by the clock. Accordingly. after looking at the hands and figures a few minutes in silence, and listen.. ing to the ticking, she said,

"I can not tell what o'clock it is, but it looks pretty late. I have a great mind to take my medicine myself."

She then turned to the table, where the lamp and the medicines were standing. The cup was there, in which Hepzibah had prepared Malleville's medicine. Malleville took it up. looked at it, and stirred it a little with the spoon.

"I wonder if this is my medicine," said she. 'I have a great mind to take it. But then, per. haps it is not my medicine. Perhaps it is poi. son."

So she put the cup down upon the table again, glad, in fact, of a plausible excuse for not taking the draught.

"I'll sit down in this rocking-chair," she said, "and wait till Hepzibah wakes up. She will wake up pretty soon."

So she went to the rocking-chair and sat down. She began to rock herself to and fro, watching the little flames and the curling smokes that were ascending from the fire. She remained thus for nearly a quarter of an hour, and then she began to be a little tired.

"What a long night!" said she. "I did not know that nights were so long. I wish that Hepzibah would wake up. But I suppose she is very tired. I mean to go and look out of the window and see if the morning is not coming Beechnut said that we could always see it coming in the east at the end of the night."

Malleville did not know which the east was, but she thought she would at any rate go and look out at the window. She accordingly went to the window, and pushing the curtains aside, and opening the shutters, she looked out. She saw the moon in the sky, and several stars, but there were no appearances of morning.

There was a bronze ink-stand upon the table, near the window, and some pens upon it. The idea occurred to Malleville that perhaps she

might write a little while to occupy the time till
Hepzibah should wake up.

"If I only had some paper," said she, "I
would write a letter to Agnes."

Malleville could not write much ; yet she had
sometimes written what she called letters, to
Phonny and to Mary Bell. Her letters were
expressed in characters partly written and partly
printed; for whenever she could not think what
the form of a letter was, as usually written with
a pen, she was accustomed to adopt the form
which she recollected to have seen in printed
books. There was another imperfection in her
writing, too, which was, that capitals and small
letters were mingled promiscuously along her
lines. So long, she thought, as the letter itself
was right, it was not very material in which of
its various forms it appeared. She was generally unfortunate, too, in her sealing, for she wet
the wafer altogether too much, and then she
was always impatient to have it stick at once,
without giving it time to get dry. And so as
she kept trying it continually, to see whether it
was sticking, and endeavoring to remedy the
difficulty, when it did not, by putting in more
wafers, wet like the first altogether too much,
the sealing was on the whole very unsuccessful,

184 BEECHNUT.

Malleville's search for note-paper. She finds it.

the whole letter being in the end very much de-
faced by the red paste with which it was exten-
sively besmeared. Still, notwithstanding these
difficulties, one of Malleville's letters, when finished, was a real letter, and it was really sealed,
and Mary Bell or Beechnut, when it was received, had no great difficulty in making out
most of the contents.

Malleville thought, therefore, that she would
now write a letter to Agnes, in accordance
with the permission which Beechnut said that
Agnes had given her. The only difficulty was
to get some note paper. She thought that
there was some in her aunt Henry's room. She
took the lamp therefore from off the stand, proceeding very carefully, so as not to waken Hepzibah, and went away with it into her aunt
Henry's room, to look.

There was a portable desk upon a table there.
Malleville set the lamp down upon the table, and
opened the portable desk. She then lifted up
the lid inside, and there she found a fine supply
of note paper of various sizes, with envelopes in
small bundles to suit. Malleville selected what
she thought was proper for her purpose, and
then putting back every thing else in good order, just as she had found i., she took the lamp

in one hand, and the note-paper and envelope
in the other, and went back into her room.
She found that Hepzibah had moved a little,
but she was sleeping as quietly as ever.

Malleville carried the lamp now to the table
by the window, and taking great care to put it
down in a place where it would not be at all in
danger of setting fire to the curtain, she took
the pen and began her writing. She worked
patiently upon her task for half an hour. The
letter was then completed. Of course it is im
possible to give any idea in a printed book of the
appearance of the writing, but the letter itself,
as Malleville intended to express it, was as follows :—

Wednesday, midnight.

DEAR AGNES:—
   I like you, because Beechnut says you like me. Please to
answer this letter.
Your affectionate friend,   M.

Malleville wrote only M. instead of her whole
name Malleville, at the bottom of her letter, because, just as she was finishing her work, the
lamp began to burn very dim. She was afraid
that it was going out. So she stopped with the
M., saying to herself, that Agnes would know
who it was from ; and, besides, if she did not,

Beechnut could tell her when he gave it to her.
She folded the note and slipped it into the envelope, and then hastily wetting a wafer, which
she found in a small compartment in the center
of the bronze inkstand, she put it in its place,
and pressed down the flap of the envelope upon
it. She then took the lamp and went to find a
pin to prick up the wick a little, to keep it from
going out

She could not find any pin, and the lamp
burned more and more dimly.

"I must go down stairs and find another
amp," said Malleville, "or else Hepzibah will
oe left all in the dark."

She turned and looked toward Hepzibah a
moment as she said this, and then added,

"Poor Hepzibah! How tired she must be to
sleep so long."

She then took the lamp, and walked softly out
of the room. The stairs creaked a little as she
descended, though she stepped as carefully as
she could. When she reached the kitchen door,
she found it shut. She opened it and went in.

The kitchen was pretty warm, as there had
been a fire in it all the day, although the fire
was now all covered up in ashes. The andirons were standing, one across the other, upon

the hearth, idle and useless. Malleville looked about the room for a lamp, but she did not see any. The kitchen was in perfect order, every thing being put properly away in its place.

"I will look into the closets," said Malleville.

So she opened a closet door and looked in. There were various articles upon the shelves, but no lamps. She then shut this door and opened another closet door, at the back side of the room. Here Malleville found four lamps standing in a row, upon the second shelf. She was very much pleased to see them. She took one of them down and carried it to the kitchen table, and then lighted it by means of a lamp-lighter, which she obtained from a lamp-lighter case hanging up by the side of the fireplace. She then blew out her own lamp, and carrying it into the closet, she put it up upon the shelf in the place of the one which she had taken away.

On the lower shelf, Malleville saw, much to her satisfaction, a plate of bread with some butter by the side of it. There was a little pitcher near, too, and Malleville, on looking into it, found that it was half full of milk.

"I am very glad that I have found this," said she, "for now I can have some supper. I wanted something, and I could not tell what. I know now. I was hungry.

She brought out the bread and butter and the milk to the kitchen-table, and then drawing up a chair, she began to eat her supper, feeling a most excellent appetite.

MALLEVILLE'S SUPPER.

She went on very prosperously for a time, having eaten two slices of bread, and drank nearly all the milk, when suddenly her attention was arrested by a movement at the head of the kitchen stairs. These stairs ascended from very near the door where Malleville had entered the kitchen, and as Malleville had left the door open, the light from her lamp shone out into the entry, and she could also, while in the kitchen, hear any sound upon the stairs. The sound which attracted her attention was like that of a person opening a door and coming out. Malleville immediately stopped drinking from her pitcher, and listened.

"Who is that down in the kitchen?" said a voice. Malleville immediately recognized the voice as that of Beechnut.

"I," said Malleville

"I?" repeated Beechnut. "Who do you mean? Is it Malleville?"

"Yes," replied Malleville.

"Why, Malleville!" exclaimed Beechnut, in a tone of profound astonishment. "What are you doing in the kitchen?"

"I am eating some supper," said Malleville.

"But, Malleville!" exclaimed Beechnut, "you ought not to be down there, eating supper at this time of night. How came you to go down?"

"Oh, I came down," replied Malleville, "to get a lamp for Hepzibah."

" For Hepzibah !" repeated Beechnut. " Did she send you down there for a lamp ?"

" Oh no,' said Malleville; " I came my-self."

" Where is Hepzibah ?" asked Beechnut.

" She is asleep," said Malleville, "and you must not speak so loud, or you will wake her up."

Malleville could now hear Beechnut laughing most immoderately, though evidently making great efforts to suppress the sound of his laugh-ter. Presently, he regained his composure in a sufficient degree to speak, and Malleville heard his voice again, calling,

" Malleville ?"

" What ?" said Malleville.

" Have you nearly finished your supper ?" asked Beechnut.

" Yes," replied Malleville. "I have only got a little more milk to drink."

" Well," said Beechnut, "when you have drank your milk, you had better go directly back to your room again, and get into bed and go to sleep."

" And what shall I do with Hepzibah ?" said Malleville.

" Where is Hepzibah ?" asked Beechnut; " is she asleep in your room ?"

"Yes," replied Malleville.

"On the sofa?" asked Beechnut.

"Yes," replied Malleville.

"Then leave her where she is," replied Beechnut "and go to bed and go to sleep. If you do
not get to sleep in half an hour, ring your bell,
and I will dress myself, and come and see what
to do."

"Well," said Malleville, "I will." So taking
her new lamp, she went up stairs again to her
room. Hepzibah was sleeping as soundly as
ever.

Malleville, in obedience to Beechnut's directions, after putting her lamp upon the stand,
went directly to her bed and lay down. She
shut up her eyes to try to go to sleep, thinking
of Beechnut's injunction to ring the bell if she
did not get to sleep in half an hour, and wondering how she was to determine when the
half hour would be ended. Long, however,
before she had decided this perplexing question,
she was fast asleep.

The next morning, Hepzibah awoke at half-
past five, which was her usual time of rising.
She started up, amazed to find that it was
morning, and that she had been asleep all night
upon the sofa in Malleville's room. Her amaze-

ment was increased at finding her feet envel
oped in a blanket, and a screen placed carefully between her face and the remains of the
fire.   She went hastily to Malleville's bedside,
and finding that the little patient was there safe
and well, she ran off to her own room, hoping
that Phonny and Beechnut would never hear
the story of her watching, and tell it to the
men ; for if they did, the men, she said to herself, would tease her almost to death about it.

When the doctor came the next morning,
and they told him about Malleville's supper, he
laughed very heartily, and said that food was
better for convalescents than physic, after all ;
and that, though patients often made very sad
mistakes in taking their case into their own
hands, yet he must admit that it proved sometimes that they could prescribe for themselves
better than the doctor.

MALLEVILLE'S FAREWELL. 193

Malleville is to return to New York.   Wallace.   His college.

CHAPTER X.

MALEVILLE'S FAREWELL.

DURING the time in which the events described
in the last few chapters took place, Phonny's
cousin Wallace was not at Franconia. He was
at college. His fall vacation was to commence
about the middle of September. It had been
arranged that he was not to come to Franconia
to spend this vacation, but to go to New York.
Malleville was to go to New York too, to spend
the vacation there with Wallace, and then afterward to return to Franconia again. Her
health and strength were gaining so steadily by
her residence in the country, that her father
and mother chose to keep her at Franconia as
much and as long as possible.

Wallace was to take Malleville with him to
New York, but he was not to come for her to
Franconia. He was to meet her on the way.
His college was in one of the interior towns of
New England, much nearer to New York than
Franconia was. The college was on the west

N

side of the Connecticut river. Franconia is on the east side. It was agreed therefore, that Beechnut should take Malleville in a small carriage, and convey her to a certain town upon the river, and that Wallace should come and meet her there.

When Phonny heard of this plan, he was very earnest to be permitted to go too. Beechnut said that *he* had no objection. Phonny then went to ask his mother. She said that she had no objection, except the expense. " You may go out," said she, " and find Beechnut, and make a calculation with him what the additional expense will be if you go ; and then come and tell me."

Phonny accordingly went out to make the calculation with Beechnut. In a short time he returned, saying that Beechnut estimated that his, that is Phonny's expenses, would be about seventy-five cents a day, and that the party would be gone a little more than three days. The total, he thought, would amount to two dollars and fifty cents.

Mrs. Henry said that that was a great deal of money to be spent upon a mere pleasure excursion for a boy, though after all it was not quite as much, she said, as she had supposed it would be. She then asked Phonny which he should prefer, the journey, or the two dollars and fifty cents to expend in play-things.

Phonny reflected upon the subject a few moments, thinking over the various ways in which such a sum could be expended, and finally concluded that he should prefer the journey. His mother then told him that he might go.

Phonny was greatly pleased with this decision. He immediately went out into the yard to find Beechnut, in order to consult with him in respect to the arrangements.

Beechnut had decided to take a certain carriage called the carryall, and two horses. There were two seats to this carryall. There was a rack for trunks and baggage behind the carryall, and this rack was so arranged, that it could be put on or taken off at pleasure. Phonny found Beechnut preparing to take the rack off.

The reason for this was, that Malleville, in her journeys back and forth, between New York and Franconia, took with her usually very little baggage. Every thing that she had at Franconia, in the way of dress, books, play-things, &c., she usually left there when she went to New York, as she had an abundant supply of all such things at home. In the same manner, when she came from New York, she usually brought very little with her, except such things as were necessary to use on the way. Beechnut knew, therefore, that a large carpet-bag would contain all that she would wish to carry, and that there would be room for this under the forward seat of the carryall.

" Mother says that I may go," said Phonny to Beechnut, " and now there is one thing that I want you to let me do."

" What is it ?" asked Beechnut.

" Will you promise that you will let me do it ?" asked Phonny.

" Yes," replied Beechnut, " if it is any thing reasonable."

Phonny then said that he wished that Beechnut would allow him to have the whole care and management of the expedition. He wished that while they were riding, Beechnut would take his seat on the back seat of the carryall, as if he were a gentleman passenger, and let Phonny sit upon the front seat with Malleville, to drive ; and when they stopped at the taverns, that Beechnut would go directly in and sit down, and leave Phonny to see that the horses were taken care of, and the dinner was ordered, and finally, when they were ready to come away, that the bill was paid. Beechnut might be ready to help him in doing any thing that he was not able to do himself, and also to assist in case of any accident, or any unexpected emergency; but in all other respects he was to travel as an indifferent spectator, leaving the whole management of the expedition to Phonny's dis-cretion.

Beechnut was at first very much in doubt in respect to the wisdom of making such an arrangement as this. He had promised to grant Phonny's request, provided that it was reasonable; but he said that there was great room to question whether this was reasonable or not. Finally, after much hesitation, he agreed to surrender the control of the expedition into Phonny's hands, until Phonny should have made *three* serious mistakes in the management of it. When Phonny should have made three such mistakes, he was then immediately to resign his power, and Beechnut was to be reinstated in his place.

By the time that this arrangement was agreed upon, Beechnut had half taken off the rack from behind the carriage. The first exercise of Phonny's power was to order it to be screwed on again. He concluded, that, although there was nothing but a carpet-bag to be carried, he would rather have that strapped on behind than to take it in under one of the seats. He thought it would look more impos ing and business-like, and more as if they were actually a party of travelers, taking a real jour- ney. Beechnut made no objection to this change, but screwed the rack on again firmly, and then brought out a long strap from the harness-room and buckled it loosely over the rack, so as to have it all ready. Phonny then directed Beechnut to have the horses harnessed and the carryall ready the next morning at eight o'clock—which was the hour that he had fixed upon as the most suitable for starting. He then left Beechnut and went into the house to find a map in order to determine, by means of it, how far it would be desirable to go the first day. He told his mother of the ar- rangement which he and Beechnut had made. She very readily acquiesced in it.

Phonny proposed to Malleville, that instead of stopping at a tavern for dinner on the first day of their journey, that they should encamp, as they had done on their expedition in search of Carlo the summer before. Malleville ap- proved this plan very highly, and Phonny began to consider what it would be best to take for provisions. He, finally, concluded upon sandwiches, cake, an apple-pie, three apples, three oranges, and a jug of milk. All these things his mother promised to have ready the following morning, with a basket to put them in. Phonny and Malleville then went out to the carryall to see where it would be best to put the basket when the provisions were packed in it.

There was a sort of box under the back seat, which opened with a lid. The lid was under the cushions. This box was a very secure place, but it was found to be too small to contain the basket. Phonny said, however, that it would be an excellent place to keep the jug of milk in.

"We will fill up the rest of the room with hay," said he, "to keep the jug from knocking about."

The children, accordingly, went out into the barn to get the hay. Phonny climbed up the ladder to the scaffold, and pulled out some of the softest hay that he could find, and threw it down to Malleville. She gathered it together in her arms as fast as Phonny threw it down, and they went back together to the carryall, taking the hay with them. They stuffed it into the box, leaving space, however, for the jug, and then shut down the lid, and put on the cushions. They decided to put their basket of provisions under the forward seat, where there was a large space; this space was open toward the front, though closed behind.

These questions being all thus settled, Phonny looked at the rack behind the carryall, and began to wish very much that they had a trunk to carry there instead of merely a carpet-bag. A carpet-bag seemed to him a very insignificant stock of baggage for three travelers going on a three days' journey;—one of them, too, as he said, a lady, setting out on a tour of four hundred miles. He asked Malleville if she could not just as well put her things in a trunk.

"Yes," said Malleville, "if my aunt Henry would only lend me one."

"And we can put my great-coat in the carpet-bag," added Phonny, "and if that is not enough, we can fill it up with hay."

Mrs. Henry said that she had no objection to lending Malleville a trunk, and she, accordingly, went up with the children into the trunk-room, which was a sort of garret, to find one

They found that most of the trunks there
were packing-trunks of monstrous size. There
were, however, two or three traveling-trunks,
and Mrs. Henry, selecting the one that she
thought most suitable, told Phonny that he and
Malleville might take it out to the head of the
stairs, and then go and ask Hepzibah to come
and carry it down for them into Malleville's
room.

Phonny and Malleville found, however, on
lifting out the trunk, that it was not at all heavy,
so they carried it down themselves. Phonny
then helped Malleville to transfer the clothes
and other articles, which had already been
packed in the carpet-bag, to the trunk. Malleville said that there were more things to be put
into it in the morning, but, notwithstanding
this, Phonny shut it up, locked it, then strapped
and buckled it carefully, and giving the key to
Malleville, he charged her to put it in her
pocket, and to be very careful to keep it there.
He was very sure, he said, that it would count
for one of his three serious mistakes, if the key
of the trunk should get left behind.

The next morning, the trunk was, of course,
unstrapped and opened again to receive the additional articles which Malleville had to put in

Hepzibah then locked and strapped it as before, giving Malleville the key.   Phonny came up to see that all was right, and then taking hold of one end of the trunk, while Hepzibah took the other, they carried it down stairs and put it in the entry, where it would be all ready to go upon the rack when the carriage should be brought to the door.

Things being thus arranged, Phonny dismissed the subject of the trunk from his mind, and turned his thoughts to the packing of his provisions for the encampment, in the basket. The basket which Mrs. Henry gave him was a square one, with a cover, but without any handle, so that it would slide very easily into its place under the seat.   When the basket was packed and put into the carriage, Phonny tried to think what else would be necessary for the journey, so as to be sure not to make one of his three mistakes in forgetting any thing at the outset.   He got a small bag of oats for the horse and put it under the front seat, by the side of the basket.   He brought out the jug of milk, and put it into the box under the back seat, among the hay; and having placed it there, as nearly as possible in the center of the box, he stuffed in more hay around it and upon the top of it, so as to make it perfectly secure. He then went to his mother to get the money to pay the expenses of the expedition. She gave it to him in a wallet, which Phonny put carefully in his pocket. The amount of the money was twenty-five dollars. It was expected that the journey would cost about ten for all three of the travelers; but Mrs. Henry always provided much more than the probable amount that would be expended on such an expedition, so that in case any accident should occur, the travelers might be prepared to meet it.

Phonny also put some books into the pockets of the carryall, that he and Malleville might have something to read by the way. Thus he thought that every thing was provided for.

He was greatly excited by all these preparations, and by the anticipated pleasures of the journey, so much so that he had very little appetite for his breakfast. After breakfast he went out into the yard, and there he found Beechnut all ready with the horses. He had harnessed them according to Phonny's directions, and now he stood by the side of them, with an unconcerned and indifferent air, as if he felt no responsibility and had nothing to do. Phonny examined the harnesses to see if all was right,

and then directed Beechnut to get in and take
the back seat. He then went all round, bid
ding every body good-bye, and finally helped
Malleville up to her place on the forward seat.
Lastly, taking the reins in his hand, he mounted
himself, and nodding once more to the people
who had assembled upon the steps to see the
party off, he drove away out of the yard.

As he came out into the road he saw a wagoner coming along with a team of four horses
and a large loaded wagon. This wagon was at
some little distance from them, but it was proceeding in the same direction in which Phonny
himself was going. Beechnut observed this
team coming, and he told Phonny that he wanted to speak with the man a moment, and asked
Phonny to let him get out for that purpose.
Phonny did so. Beechnut accordingly descended from the carryall, walked back to the wagon,
and after conversing a minute or two with the
wagoner, he returned. Phonny asked him
what it was that he went to see the wagoner
about. Beechnut replied, that it was only a
little business about some teaming that the wagoner was going to do for him.

"Now," said Phonny, "we are fairly started.
Have I not managed pretty well, Beechnut?"

"Very well, indeed," said Beechnut.

After proceeding about a mile, the attention of Phonny and Malleville was attracted by a group of girls standing under the trees at a corner where two roads met. Each of the girls had a bouquet in her hand. On approaching nearer, Malleville found that it was a party of her friends, headed by Mary Bell, who had come out to that point to intercept her on the way, and bid her good-bye. The flowers which they held in their hands were for Malleville, as parting presents.

FAREWELL TO MALLEVILLE.

Phonny stopped the carryall when he came to the spot, and the girls began to climb up eagerly to Malleville in the wagon, to kiss her and bid her good-bye. They gave her their bouquets too, and at first Malleville was embarrassed to know what to do with so many flowers. Mary Bell, however, relieved her of this difficulty by pinning the bouquets up in the inside of the carryall, some on one side and some on the other. As the bouquets were formed generally of highly colored autumnal flowers, they gave to the interior of the carryall, when arranged in their places, a very gay and brilliant appearance. When all was ready, Malleville bade Mary Bell and her other friends good-bye, receiving many charges from them to come back again to Franconia as soon as possible, and then Phonny drove on.

The party had a very pleasant ride, and met with a great variety of incidents and adventures, which can not here be particularly described. The children enjoyed every moment of the journey, and nothing whatever occurred to mar their pleasure except that Phonny at one time, when he got out to walk up a hill, was extremely frightened at observing that there was no trunk upon the rack. He im-

mediately exclaimed in a tone of extreme sur-
prise,

" Why, Beechnut! We have lost off our
trunk!"

" Have we ?" said Beechnut.

Beechnut was riding at his ease on the back
seat of the carryall, and he seemed to pay very
little attention to Phonny's announcement. He
did not even look round.

Phonny ran forward and called upon Malleville to stop the horses, and with a countenance
of great excitement and anxiety, he asked Beechnut what they should do.

" I don't know," said Beechnut, carelessly.
" I am only a passenger."

" We might turn round and go back," said
Phonny, " and perhaps we should find it in the
road. I wonder how long ago it fell off!"

" Perhaps some robbers cut it off," said
Beechnut.

" I don't think *that* is very likely," replied
Phonny.

" I think it is quite as likely as that it fell
off," replied Beechnut, " that is, if you strapped
it on strong."

" *I* did not strap it on," said Phonny. " *You*
strapped it on."

" Did I ?" said Beechnut.

" Yes," said Phonny,—" I suppose so." Then
he paused, hesitating, and tried to recollect
whether the trunk was put on or not. He
finally concluded that it had been left at home.
For a moment he seemed to be in great trouble.

" What shall I do ?" said he to Beechnut.
' You were to help me in case of any difficulty,
and this is a difficulty, I am sure."

" Well," said Beechnut, " I will help you. In
the first place, I advise you not to be anxious or
frightened about this trouble. You did the best
that you possibly could do, and tried to attend
to every thing necessary in the setting out.
You gave all your time and thoughts to the
work, and made most faithful endeavors ; and
if among the multiplicity of things that you had
to do, one escaped you, you are not to blame.
Considering that it is the first time that you un-
dertook to take such a charge, you have done
remarkably well. And then, besides, leaving
the trunk behind is no very serious misfortune
after all."

Phonny was greatly comforted by these
words. He still, however, seemed somewhat
perplexed, and he asked Beechnut what he
should do.

" There are three things that you can do,"
replied Beechnut. " First, you can go back
and get the trunk; secondly, you can go on
without it; and thirdly, you can put the case
into *my* hands, and so dismiss all thoughts of it
from your mind."

" Well," said Phonny, " I will do that
last."

"Only," continued Beechnut, "we must
count the leaving of the trunk as one of your
three mistakes."

" Yes," said Phonny, "I agree to that."

" Very well," said Beechnut, "then drive
on."

Phonny wished very much to know what
Beechnut was going to do, but Beechnut did
not seem inclined to answer any questions, except to say that he would contrive some way
or other to get out of the difficulty.

Phonny, accordingly, dismissed all thought
and care in respect to the lost trunk from his
mind, and drove on as before, enjoying his ride
very highly until twelve o'clock, when the
whole party stopped at a place of encampment,
which Phonny selected in a wild and romantic
spot, under a group of rocks by the side of
a mountain stream. While the party were

O

eating their dinner here, they heard the noise of wheels coming along the road, and presently, the great wagon which they had seen just as they were leaving home, came into view. The wagoner nodded to Beechnut as he passed.

" All right?" said Beechnut, in a tone of inquiry.

" All right," responded the wagoner, in a tone of reply.

Phonny wanted to know what Beechnut meant by that dialogue with the wagoner. But Beechnut did not seem inclined to explain it. On the other hand, his countenance assumed a very mysterious expression, indicating that there was some deep understanding between him and the wagoner.

"It is about the trunk," said Phonny, "I verily believe. Isn't it, Beechnut?"

" Ah!" said Beechnut, "now you have found me out."

Beechnut then confessed that the wagoner had the trunk in his wagon. He had perceived that Phonny was coming away without it, and so had secretly requested the wagoner to bring it along.

Phonny made no more mistakes after this, but managed the business that devolved upon

him in conducting the journey in a very satisfactory manner.   He delivered Malleville safely
into Wallace's hands at the appointed place of
meeting, and then he drove Beechnut back to
Franconia.

THE END.

BOOKS BY THE ABBOTTS.

THE FRANCONIA STORIES.

By Jacob Abbott. In Ten Volumes. Beautifully Illustrated. 18mo, Cloth, 90 cents per Vol.; the set complete in case, $9 00.

1. Malleville.
2. Mary Bell.
3. Ellen Linn.
4. Wallace.
5. Beechnut.
6. Stuyvesant.
7. Agnes.
8. Mary Erskine.
9. Rodolphus.
10. Caroline.

MARCO PAUL SERIES.

Marco Paul's Voyages and Travels in the Pursuit of Knowledge. By Jacob Abbott. Beautifully Illustrated. Complete in 6 Volumes, 16mo, Cloth, 90 cents per Volume. Price of the set, in case, $5 40.

In New York.
On the Erie Canal.
In the Forests of Maine.
In Vermont.
In Boston.
At the Springfield Armory.

RAINBOW AND LUCKY SERIES.

By Jacob Abbott. Beautifully Illustrated. 16mo, Cloth, 90 cents each. The set complete, in case, $4 50.

Handie.
Rainbow's Journey.
The Three Pines.
Selling Lucky.
Up the River.

YOUNG CHRISTIAN SERIES.

By Jacob Abbott. In Four Volumes. Richly Illustrated with Engravings, and Beautifully Bound. 12mo, Cloth. $1 75 per Vol. The set complete, Cloth, $7 00, in Half Calf, $14 00.

1. The Young Christian.
2. The Corner Stone.
3. The Way to Do Good.
4. Hoaryhead and M'Donner

HARPER'S STORY BOOKS.

A Series of Narratives, Biographies, and Tales, for the Instruction and Entertainment of the Young. By JACOB ABBOTT. Embellished with more than One Thousand beautiful Engravings. Square 4to, complete in 12 large Volumes, or 36 small ones.

"HARPER'S STORY BOOKS" can be obtained complete in Twelve Volumes, bound in blue and gold, each one containing Three Stories, for $21 00, or in Thirty-six thin Volumes, bound in crimson and gold, each containing One Story, for $32 40. The volumes may be had separately—the large ones at $1 75 each, the others at 90 cents each.

VOL. I.

BRUNO; or, Lessons of Fidelity, Patience, and Self-Denial Taught by a Dog.

WILLIE AND THE MORTGAGE: showing How Much may be Accomplished by a Boy.

THE STRAIT GATE; or, The Rule of Exclusion from Heaven.

VOL. II.

THE LITTLE LOUVRE; or, The Boys' and Girls' Picture-Gallery.

PRANK; or, The Philosophy of Tricks and Mischief.

EMMA; or, The Three Misfortunes of a Belle.

VOL. III.

VIRGINIA; or, A Little Light on a Very Dark Saying.

TIMBOO AND JOLIBA; or, The Art of Being Useful.

TIMBOO AND FANNY; or, The Art of Self-Instruction.

VOL. IV.

THE HARPER ESTABLISHMENT; or, How the Story Books are Made.

FRANKLIN, the Apprentice-Boy.

THE STUDIO; or, Illustrations of the Theory and Practice of Drawing, for Young Artists at Home.

VOL. V.

THE STORY OF ANCIENT HISTORY, from the Earliest Periods to the Fall of the Roman Empire.

THE STORY OF ENGLISH HISTORY, from the Earliest Periods to the American Revolution.

THE STORY OF AMERICAN HISTORY, from the Earliest Settlement of the Country to the Establishment of the Federal Constitution.

VOL. VI.

JOHN TRUE; or, The Christian Experience of an Honest Boy.

ELFRED; or, The Blind Boy and his Pictures.

THE MUSEUM; or, Curiosities Explained.

VOL. VII.

THE ENGINEER; or, How to Travel in the Woods.

RAMBLES AMONG THE ALPS.

THE THREE GOLD DOLLARS; or, An Account of the Adventures of Robin Green.

VOL. VIII.

THE GIBRALTAR GALLERY; being an Account of various Things both Curious and Useful.

THE ALCOVE: containing some Farther Account of Timboo, Mark, and Fanny.

DIALOGUES for the Amusement and Instruction of Young Persons.

VOL. IX.

THE GREAT ELM; or, Robin Green and Josiah Lane at School.

AUNT MARGARET; or, How John True kept his Resolutions.

VERNON; or, Conversations about Old Times in England.

VOL. X.

CARL AND JOCKO; or, The Adventures of the Little Italian Boy and his Monkey.

LAPSTONE; or, The Sailor turned Shoemaker.

ORKNEY, THE PEACEMAKER; or, The Various Ways of Settling Disputes.

VOL. XI.

JUDGE JUSTIN; or, The Little Court of Morningdale.

MINIGO; or, The Fairy of Cairnstone Abbey.

JASPER; or, The Spoiled Child Recovered.

VOL. XII.

CONGO; or, Jasper's Experience in Command.

VIOLA and her Little Brother Arno.

LITTLE PAUL; or, How to be Patient in Sickness and Pain.

Some of the Story Books are written particularly for girls, and some for Boys, and the different Volumes are adapted to various ages, so that the work forms a *Complete Library of Story Books* for all the Children of the Family and the Sunday-School.

ABBOTTS' ILLUSTRATED HISTORIES.

Biographical Histories.   By JACOB ABBOTT and JOHN S.
C. ABBOTT.   The Volumes of this Series are printed and
bound uniformly, and are embellished with numerous Engravings.   16mo, Cloth, $1 00 per volume.   Price of the set (32
vols.), $32 00.

A series of volumes containing severally full accounts of the lives,
characters, and exploits of the most distinguished sovereigns, po-
tentates, and rulers that have been chiefly renowned among man-
kind, in the various ages of the world, from the earliest periods to
the present day.

The successive volumes of the series, though they each contain
the life of a single individual, and constitute thus a distinct and in-
dependent work, follow each other in the main, in regular historical
order, and each one continues the general narrative of history down
to the period at which the next volume takes up the story; so that
the whole series presents to the reader a connected narrative of the
line of general history from the present age back to the remotest
times.

The narratives are intended to be succinct and comprehensive, and
are written in a very plain and simple style.   They are, however, not
juvenile in their character, nor intended exclusively for the young.
The volumes are sufficiently large to allow each history to comprise
all the leading facts in the life of the personage who is the subject
of it, and thus to communicate all the information in respect to him
which is necessary for the purposes of the general reader.

Such being the design and character of the works, they would
seem to be specially adapted, not only for family reading, but also
for district, town, school, and Sunday-school libraries, as well as for
text-books in literary seminaries.

The plan of the series, and the manner in which the design has
been carried out by the author in the execution of it, have been highly commended by the press in all parts of the country.   The whole
series has been introduced into the school libraries of several of the
largest and most influential states.

ABRAHAM LINCOLN'S OPINION OF ABBOTTS' HISTORIES.—*In a conversation with the President just before his death, Mr. Lincoln said:* "*I
want to thank you and your brother for Abbotts' series of Histories.   I
have not education enough to appreciate the profound works of volu-
minous historians; and if I had, I have no time to read them.   But
your series of Histories gives me, in brief compass, just that knowledge
of past men and events which I need.   I have read them with the greatest interest.   To them I am indebted for about all the historical knowledge I have.*"

CYRUS THE GREAT.

DARIUS THE GREAT.

XERXES.

ALEXANDER THE GREAT.

ROMULUS.

HANNIBAL.

PYRRHUS.

JULIUS CÆSAR.

CLEOPATRA.

NERO.

ALFRED THE GREAT.

WILLIAM THE CONQUEROR.

RICHARD I.

RICHARD II.

RICHARD III.

MARY QUEEN OF SCOTS.

QUEEN ELIZABETH.

CHARLES I.

CHARLES II.

JOSEPHINE.

MARIA ANTOINETTE.

MADAME ROLAND.

HENRY IV.

PETER THE GREAT.

GENGHIS KHAN.

KING PHILIP.

HERNANDO CORTEZ.

MARGARET OF ANJOU.

JOSEPH BONAPARTE.

QUEEN HORTENSE.

LOUIS XIV.

LOUIS PHILIPPE.

THE LITTLE LEARNER SERIES.

A Series for Very Young Children. Designed to Assist in the Earliest Development of the Mind of a Child, while under its Mother's Special Care, during the first Five or Six Years of its Life. By JACOB ABBOTT. Beautifully Illustrated. Complete in 5 Small 4to Volumes, Cloth, 90 cents per Vol. Price of the set, in case, $4 50.

———

LEARNING TO TALK; or, Entertaining and Instructive Lessons in the Use of Language. 170 Engravings.

LEARNING TO THINK : consisting of Easy and Entertaining Lessons, designed to Assist in the First Unfolding of the Reflective and Reasoning Powers of Children. 120 Engravings.

LEARNING TO READ; consisting of Easy and Entertaining Lessons, designed to Assist Young Children in Studying the Forms of the Letters, and in beginning to Read. 160 Engravings.

LEARNING ABOUT COMMON THINGS; or, Familiar Instruction for Children in respect to the Objects around them that attract their Attention and awaken their Curiosity in the Earliest Years of Life. 120 Engravings.

LEARNING ABOUT RIGHT AND WRONG; or, Entertaining and Instructive Lessons for Young Children in respect to their Duty. 90 Engravings.

KINGS AND QUEENS; or, Life in the Palace: consisting of Historical Sketches of Josephine and Maria Louisa, Louis Philippe, Ferdinand of Austria, Nicholas, Isabella II., Leopold, Victoria, and Louis Napoleon. By John S. C. Abbott. Illustrated. 12mo, Cloth, $1 75.

A SUMMER IN SCOTLAND: a Narrative of Observations and Adventures made by the Author during a Summer spent among the Glens and Highlands in Scotland. By Jacob Abbott. Illustrated. 12mo, Cloth, $1 75.

THE ROMANCE OF SPANISH HISTORY. By John S. C. Abbott. Illustrated. 12mo, Cloth, $2 00.

THE TEACHER. Moral Influences Employed in the Instruction and Government of the Young. By Jacob Abbott. Illustrated. 12mo, Cloth, $1 75.

GENTLE MEASURES IN TRAINING THE YOUNG. Gentle Measures in the Management and Training of the Young; or, The Principles on which a Firm Parental Authority may be Established and Maintained without Violence or Anger, and the Right Development of the Moral and Mental Capacities be Promoted by Methods in Harmony with the Structure and the Characteristics of the Juvenile Mind. A Book for the Parents of Young Children. By Jacob Abbott. Illustrated. 12mo, Cloth, $1 75.

SCIENCE
FOR THE YOUNG.

By JACOB ABBOTT.

WITH ILLUSTRATIONS.

HEAT. 12mo, Cloth, $1 50.
LIGHT. 12mo, Cloth, $1 50.
WATER AND LAND. 12mo, Cloth, $1 50.
FORCE. 12mo, Cloth, $1 50.

Few men enjoy a wider or better earned popularity as a writer for the young than Jacob Abbott. His series of histories, and stories illustrative of moral truths, have furnished amusement and instruction to thousands. He has the knack of piquing and gratifying curiosity. In the book before us he shows his happy faculty of imparting useful information through the medium of a pleasant narrative, keeping alive the interest of the young reader, and fixing in his memory valuable truths.—*Mercury,* New Bedford, Mass.

Jacob Abbott is almost the only writer in the English language who knows how to combine real amusement with real instruction in such a manner that the eager young readers are quite as much interested in the useful knowledge he imparts as in the story which he makes so pleasant a medium of instruction.—*Buffalo Commercial Advertiser.*

* * * Mr. Abbott has avoided the errors so common with writers for popular effect, that of slurring over the difficulties of the subject through the desire of making it intelligible and attractive to unlearned readers. He never tampers with the truth of science, nor attempts to dodge the solution of a knotty problem behind a cloud of plausible illustrations.—*N. Y. Tribune.*

POPULAR HISTORIES

BY

JOHN S. C. ABBOTT.

HISTORY OF FREDERICK THE GREAT.

The History of Frederick the Second, called Frederick the Great. By JOHN S. C. ABBOTT. Elegantly Illustrated. 8vo, Cloth, $5 00.

THE FRENCH REVOLUTION.

The French Revolution of 1789, as Viewed in the Light of Republican Institutions. By JOHN S. C. ABBOTT. With 100 Engravings. 8vo, Cloth, $5 00.

NAPOLEON BONAPARTE.

The History of Napoleon Bonaparte. By JOHN S. C. ABBOTT. With Maps, Woodcuts, and Portraits on Steel. 2 vols., 8vo, Cloth, $10 00.

NAPOLEON AT ST. HELENA.

Napoleon at St. Helena; or, Interesting Anecdotes and Remarkable Conversations of the Emperor during the Five and a Half Years of his Captivity. Collected from the Memorials of Las Casas, O'Meara, Montholon, Antommarchi, and others. By JOHN S. C. ABBOTT. With Illustrations. 8vo, Cloth, $5 00.

By JOHN S. C. ABBOTT.

CHILD AT HOME.

The Child at Home; or, the Principles of Filial Duty familiarly Illustrated. By JOHN S. C. ABBOTT. Woodcuts.
16mo, Cloth, $1 00.

The duties and trials peculiar to the child are explained and illustrated in this volume in the same clear and attractive manner
in which those of the mother are set forth in the "Mother at Home."
These two works may be considered as forming a complete manual
of filial and maternal relations.

MOTHER AT HOME.

The Mother at Home; or, the Principles of Maternal Duty
familiarly Illustrated. By JOHN S. C. ABBOTT. Engravings. 16mo, Cloth, $1 00.

This book treats of the important questions of maternal responsibility and authority; of the difficulties which the mother will experience, the errors to which she is liable, the methods and plans
she should adopt; of the religious instruction which she should
impart, and of the results which she may reasonably hope will follow her faithful and persevering exertions. These subjects are
illustrated with the felicity characteristic of all the productions of
the author.

PRACTICAL CHRISTIANITY.

Practical Christianity. A Treatise specially designed for
Young Men. By JOHN S. C. ABBOTT. 16mo, Cloth,
$1 00.

It is characterized by the simplicity of style and appositeness of
illustration which make a book easily read and readily understood.
It is designed to instruct and interest young men in the effectual
truths of Christianity. It comes down to their plane of thought,
and, in a genial, conversational way, strives to lead them to a life
of godliness.—*Watchman and Reflector*.

It abounds in wise and practical suggestions.—*N. Y. Commercial
Advertiser*.